Park's Lot

Willow Springs Ranch: V

Laura Harner

Park's Lot is a work of fiction. Names, characters, places, and incidents are the product of the author's imagination or are used fictitiously. Any resemblance to actual persons, living or dead, events, or locales is entirely coincidental.

Contents

Acknowledgements

A special thank you to Will Parkinson, Jae Ashley, and Dan Skinner. Your advice, inspiration, and input are invaluable.

The author acknowledges the trademarked status and trademark owners of the following trademarks mentioned in this work of fiction:

Boy Scout: Boy Scouts of America Corporation
Creamsicle: Conopco, Inc.
Star Trek: Paramount Pictures Corporation
In-N-Out Burger: In-N-Out Burgers Corporation
Volkswagen: Volkswagen Aktiengesellschaft Corporation
CamelBak: CamelBak Products, LLC
Grateful Dead: Grateful Dead Productions Corporation

Chapter One

"No. This is getting out of control—I already told you we aren't going to drive through the In-N-Out Burger. I think two weeks of dispersed camping is exactly what you two need. It's time you learned you don't get your own way all the time."

There was no response from the back as the orange and white vintage VW bus, sped past the Kingman exit. Thirty minutes later, Park Williams took a random exit, turned left, and headed straight for the undesignated Bureau of Land Management acreage. Ignoring the whimpering from the back, he bypassed the first two gravel roads and took the third—just because it felt right. Pinyon and juniper dotted the hilly landscape, and he could see the Prescott mountain range in the distance. The blue sky hung heavy over it all, as wide open as you could find anywhere.

"All right, you two. It's time to look for our new home. Well, our new home for the next two weeks. Do you want to stay on the north side of the road or the south side? And let me tell you something, Scooby. If you don't stay around the tent, then I'm going to put you on your leash. Do I make myself clear, young man?"

With renewed whimpering, the two dogs began to jump around the back of the van. With Scooby, that wasn't a problem. Six pounds of attitude tended to not make much of a dent in Park's belongings. Taco, on the other hand, weighed one seventy-five and could wipe out a weeks' worth of groceries with one sweep of his tail.

The graded road continued on to the south as far as Park could see, however, there was a smaller offshoot to the east just up ahead. It looked like it might have been a fire road. This was exactly the type of camping that Park liked best. Miles from anywhere, no people around, just him and the boys, a couple of good books and his sketchpad. Usually there were canvases too, but since he rarely tried to paint while he was living out of his van, he'd left them in storage. Making a decision, he took the left turn onto the narrower road.

"Scooby, stop it. You're winding Taco up. Taco, sit down. Oh for fuck's sake."

There was a sudden splash as one of the water containers burst open under Taco's weight. Park pulled off the road, putting his van between two sprawling junipers. After stopping the engine, he jumped out of the van and ran around to the side to open the door. The dogs spilled out even as Park climbed in to try to save as much of the water as possible.

When you elected to do remote camping, the only water supply involved driving back to town to buy more bottles. Losing a gallon or two wasn't going to hurt, but he would sure hate to have to go back to town any sooner than necessary.

Finding his perfect campsite involved a scouting mission, especially since the dogs had been cooped up for hours and needed to burn off some energy, so he reached for his hydration pack. After dropping a few protein bars inside the pocket, he slipped into the straps and threaded the tube over his shoulder. After an experimental suck on the mouthpiece to ensure the water would flow and there were no crimps in the tubing, Park exited his van. Time to find a camping spot to call home for the next two weeks.

Taco sat at the front of the van, quivering with excitement, his need to run barely restrained. Scooby was nowhere in sight. Typical.

"Come on, Taco, show me where Scooby went."

As if he'd fired a starting pistol, Taco took off, heading away from the road, clearly with a destination in mind. Hopefully, they were heading in the right direction because a dog Scooby's size wasn't much more than vulture bait out here.

"Scooby!" With a grin and a sigh, Park jogged after his boys, knowing they were all three happy to be out of the van. As long as they made their way back before sundown everything would be just fine. They could even wait until tomorrow to set up their campsite. It wouldn't be the first time they'd slept inside the van together.

Losing sight of both dogs, he could hear them barking at each other, and knew he was on the right track, so he slowed and reached into the pocket of his faded jeans to remove a blue and gold scrunchie. Although his hair was already in a tail, the typical springtime desert breeze was kicking up gusts that had loose strands sticking to his face. After weaving his hair into a tight braid, he secured it then carefully picked his way through Manzanita, scrub oak, and claret cactus covering the ground.

"Come on, Taco—Scooby? Where are you guys?" He stopped to listen and thought he heard the big dog whimpering. *Oh shit.* Possibilities started to play through his mind as he ran full on toward the sound of his barking dogs. Hopefully the big lug had just gotten turned around and couldn't find Scooby. Although, he could have brushed into one of the cholla cactus. The little branches broke off and stuck tenaciously with just the briefest contact. Or something much worse, like last time, when he'd found a snake... Definitely not good. Maybe Park should reconsider getting a pellet gun, which he could use to kick up rocks or maybe something that would make a big noise and scare any two or four-legged creatures away from their campsite.

He finally caught sight of Taco and Scooby on the far side of a trio of junipers that must be hundreds of years old based on the diameter of their trunks. The trees formed a canopy, providing shelter and a soft bed of dirt. The indigenous people would have stopped here, maybe stayed for a while before resuming their nomadic travels.

Taco nuzzled at something, whimpered again, then sat back on his haunches. Park slowed to a walk, unsure of what the big dog was doing.

"Taco? Scooby? Come here, boys."

At the sound of Park's voice, the Great Dane stood and the Chihuahua began to dance in a circle around the bigger dog, yapping wildly, an excited and very vocal jumping bean.

"What do you have there, boy?" Park asked as he slowly approached the bundle in a heap. A low moan sent his heart racing. "Jesus fucking Christ." He raced forward and fell to his knees at what appeared to be the bloody broken body of a man.

Unsure of what to touch first, he raked the body over with his gaze. Brown hiking boots, khaki and olive green canvas hunting pants and shirt, a bloody and dirt matted cheek, eyes swollen closed. Through dried, cracked lips came a whispered groan.

"Help," the man sighed.

Removing his hydration pack, Park held it over the parched lips and let a few drops of water drizzle into his mouth. "Hey there. I'm going to help you. Let's get some water into you first, then I'm going to try to see where you're hurt. Can you tell me your name?"

9

"Hurt," the man repeated. The tip of a pale pink tongue appeared at the crease of his mouth and Park drizzled more water, coating his tongue with life-sustaining fluid. He didn't know how long this man had been out here, but regardless of what injuries he had, without water, there could be no life.

"I know you're hurt. I'm going to get you help. Let's just see how bad you're injured. I don't have my phone with me and it's at least a mile back to my van." He drizzled more water, then starting at the man's feet, he ran his hands firmly over muscular legs, along narrow hips, pressed against the flat stomach, waist, and right arm. "Other than that nice big gasp you gave when I touched your thigh, does anything else on this side hurt?"

"No."

"Think you can turn over or are you laying on some injuries I need to know about?"

The man's body rocked slightly as if he tried to turn. Park gripped his shoulder and helped him roll onto his back. More blood dotted the man's neck and open collar of his shirt, but the blood seemed to be from the numerous scrapes and scratches rather than from a significant wound. Park finished checking his left side and found nothing to make him think there were broken bones.

"Here's what I see, big man. You have a head injury that appears to have bled heavily at some point, but has stopped bleeding now. I can't tell whether that's due to how long it's been since you banged your noggin, the dirt bandage you're sporting, or loss of blood. I don't see any other evidence of major wounds. Without moving you, there's no real way to tell the extent of your injuries. I think the best we can do is for me to hike back to my van and try for some cell phone reception. I don't know if they can get an ambulance out this far or if you need to be medevaced to Kingman. Let's get you some more water before I leave."

A surprisingly strong hand gripped Park's wrist and held tight. "No."

"There is not much I can do here for you. You need medical attention."

"No doctor. Help me up."

"Honey, I can help you sit up, but trust me when I say you aren't going anywhere." Suiting words to action, Park reached his hand underneath the broad shoulders and helped the man sit up. He kept his arm in place to prevent him from tilting straight on over. With the other hand, he put the mouthpiece from his hydration pack between chiseled lips.

"Drink some more, but not too fast. We don't want to have you puking. Now, what did you say your name was, honey?"

After a few swallows, the man's lips parted and the mouthpiece fell away. Park snatched it before it fell to the ground and got dirty.

"Tanner," he said in a scratchy voice. "Name's Tanner."

"Nice to meet you, Tanner. My name is Park. Can you tell me what happened to you?" Given the man's location and camouflage outfit, Park was pretty sure he was looking at some type of a hunting accident. However, the explanation wasn't nearly as important as assessing Tanner's ability to hold a conversation and remain upright. He gave the stranger another long pull on the water tube before removing it once again so he could answer the question.

"I don't— I'm not sure what happened. Someone…hit me?" The man blinked then slowly turned his head to look around. "Don't remember how I got here."

"Judging from the scratches on your hand and chest, I'm going to guess you crawled," Park said. "I don't see anything around here that looks like a campsite. Were you hunting?"

"I don't— I don't think so. Do you have any food?"

Park smiled. If the man was in good enough condition to be hungry, then the injuries were likely not life-threatening. It also made him wonder once again just how long it had been since he'd sustained the injury. Head wounds were notorious bleeders. The injury on the side of Tanner's head was roughly the size of a softball, swollen and matted with red sandy soil. Deep purple marks around the edges faded to greens and yellows the farther he got from the initial injury. The wound could be several days old. Just beyond the cover of the trees there was a path that looked as if someone had dragged something heavy over the sandy rocks. Whether Tanner had dragged himself or someone had done it for him was the question, wasn't it?

Retrieving a protein bar from the pocket of his CamelBak hydration pack, Park opened the package and held it as even, white teeth bit down. Tanner chewed and then swallowed hard.

"Here, take another sip of water." Together, they continued the small-bite-small-drink process until Tanner had consumed the first bar and close to a quart of water. "Okay, Tanner, I think maybe you're going to be okay if we can get you up against one of these trees. You can sit here while I go call for help. I'll leave you my water bag and another bar."

Scooby yapped and danced around in a circle, drawing his attention for a moment. "Oh, yeah, thanks, Scoobs." He turned back to find Tanner staring at him. "I'll leave Taco with you, as well. Don't go anywhere." He kept his tone light.

Tanner started to shake his head then closed his eyes and listed left, before straightening himself once again. "No. I don't know exactly…" He blinked slowly, then met Park's gaze. "I think I'm better off staying here. No hospital. If you could leave me some more water and a couple of bars, I'll be okay."

"Like hell you will. I don't even know how you stayed alive in the nighttime temperatures if you were here overnight. I can't leave you out here. Why don't you want to go to town? Are you some kind a fugitive on the run?"

Tanner blinked again. "I don't think so. I just don't remember how I got here. I think maybe…this is going to sound crazy, but I think someone tried to kill me. I need to think about this before I go anywhere. If you can leave me a little food and water before you go…" he repeated.

"Yeah, you're right. That does sound crazy. Not the part about someone trying to kill you because I can invent seven reasons to Sunday for a good murder. But there is no way in hell I could walk away and leave you out here with nothing but a protein bar and a bag of water. So what's it going to be? Are you coming with me or am I staying here with you?"

****

Tanner stared at the stubborn set of the jaw on the blond-haired, blue-eyed man in front of him. He definitely did not feel up to an argument and who the fuck did this stranger think he was, anyway? Park? What the hell kind of name was Park? He needed to convince the man to go away and leave him alone. Disturbing images were floating just on the edge of his vision and he needed time to sort things out. Like did he really remember his brother T-bone swinging a baseball bat in the direction of his head? It was there at the periphery, like maybe he'd turned his head at the last minute…or maybe it was a shadow as

14

someone came up from behind. No doubt T-bone was a snake, but he needed to be really sure that that was a true memory and not some leftover dark dream based on his brother's penchant for violence.

If T-bone really had crossed that line and was willing to try to kill Tanner? Well, he sure as hell couldn't go home now, could he? Especially if the other memory floating around in his jumbled brain was true. Had he really been trying to wave down the approaching WSR cowboy? Even more important, had he been lying in wait to ambush somebody? The problem was he just couldn't trust his memories, not yet. He needed food, water, rest. And he sure as hell needed it without the damned yapping dog and his too pretty owner.

"Look, Park… Right?" He waited, prepared to say whatever he needed to make his rescuer leave.

Park held up a hand and his eyes crinkled at the corners to match his smile. "Stop. I can already tell you decided to try the reasonable approach with me. You might as well save your breath. I have nowhere I need to be except right here. I planned to camp somewhere off grid for the next two weeks, at least, so I might as well pick this spot if you refuse to go to town for medical care."

"Shit." Tanner brought a shaky hand up and started to feel around the edges of his wound. Wincing, he deliberately ignored knowledge that he should probably have some medical treatment for the side of his face that was currently throbbing and threatening to take on a life of its own. However, until he knew more about how he got here—and why—he wasn't budging. So if this long-haired pretty boy wanted to camp out here in the middle of the chaparral, so be it. He was not up to a prolonged discussion.

As if he'd offered another argument, Park cut him off before he could say anything further. "Save it, Rambo, I can see your mind working a mile a minute, but I'm not going anywhere. Well, except I'm going to my van. You keep the water. Here are two more protein bars, and I'm leaving Taco to guard over you. Scooby might stay, too, but there's no real telling with him. He tends to go wherever he thinks he's the most needed or the most important."

Tanner looked at the large brindle-colored Great Dane. "Scooby, huh?"

Park shook his head, the long braid swinging back and forth over his shoulders, and made a clicking noise with his tongue. "You should know to never stereotype. That is Taco," he said with a grin that nearly took Tanner's breath away. He nodded toward the small Chihuahua who couldn't possibly weigh more than five or six pounds. "That's Scooby."

Despite himself, Tanner chuffed a small laugh, then closed his eyes as a sharp pain hit him in the vicinity of his left rib cage. "Ouch."

Park shook his head and looked like he wanted to say something more about taking Tanner to the hospital. Instead, the slender man pushed to his feet and began walking away, leaving Tanner staring at a tight ass in faded jeans. *God.* What was wrong with him that he could think of being with a man? Especially at a time like this.

As if he felt the gaze, Park stopped and turned to face him. "It's an easy walk back to the van, but I need to load up what I can carry. It will probably take me three or four trips to get what we need for tonight. Tomorrow, we'll see how you're feeling and if you still refuse to let me take you to Kingman, then I'll go get the rest of my stuff. Taco, stay—guard." With that, the strange angel walked away, but with a promise he would return.

Chapter Two

Park pounded the last of the tent stakes with his mallet, then walked around to check his work. Satisfied everything was aligned, he attached the guy-wires, then called it a job well done. Between the hammering and the four trips to his van and back, Park's arms were shaky and his legs felt like a couple of noodles.

Glancing over at his temporary roommate, Park blinked in surprise. After the second trip, Park had rolled out one of the sleeping bags on top of a tarp and helped Tanner move to a more comfortable spot. Now Tanner was stretched out on his left side, one hand tucked under his cheek, his face slack underneath the blood and bruises. Taco was on the sleeping bag, back-to-back with Tanner, stretched to his full-length, and snoring softly. Scooby was curled up next to Tanner's stomach, watching Park work, perfectly comfortable with the stranger.

Although Scooby and Taco had plenty of experience meeting new people, they rarely cuddled with anyone except Park. His mother believed dogs could sense a good heart. She would no doubt say, if they liked Tanner, then he had to be a good person. Time would tell. There was still that little matter of how the man had been hurt and why he didn't want to go back to Kingman.

Between each of his treks, he'd checked on Tanner, spending a few minutes making sure the man drank water and that his wound wasn't showing fresh signs of bleeding. Now it was time to build the fire so he could boil water to clean the wound. Growing up with hippie parents taught you a lot about self-sufficiency and homeopathic cures.

In principle, it didn't bother him in the least that they would stay in the wilderness to treat Tanner's injuries. More infections were caused by medical staff and in hospitals than by contact with the everyday world.

Forming a small ring of stones first, Park used his shovel to dig out a fire pit. He collected small sticks for kindling and larger branches, and then set up two folding camp chairs near the perimeter of the fire.

"I'm sorry," Tanner's voice creaked out.

"Hey there, Rambo. How are you feeling?" Park walked around the fire and hunched down in front of Tanner.

"Uhm…better, I think. Much better. Thank you for everything you've done. If you hadn't come along when you did—"

"That wasn't me, that was all Scooby." Park smiled as Tanner looked over his shoulder at the Great Dane. "A common mistake, Scooby's the Chihuahua. I did tell you earlier but I don't think you were quite with us yet. The big guy behind you is Taco."

Tanner rested his hand on Scooby's back and scratched lightly behind his ears, even as he looked over his shoulder. "Nice to meet you, Taco. You make a mighty fine blanket."

"I imagine he kept you pretty warm this afternoon. However, as soon as the sun goes down, it's going to get damned cold out here. If you think you're up to it, I'd like to move you closer to the fire and get a good look at that head injury. It needs to be cleaned."

"Yeah, I'm ready to try sitting up again." He patted Scooby's head once more, then put his hand on the ground and pushed himself upright. Taco jumped up, instantly alert, sniffing the air as if he could identify the disturbance that woke him from his slumber.

Tanner laughed and it was a very good sound. Park stood and put a hand out. Tanner clasped the offered hand and Park pulled him to his feet. *Wow.* Tanner towered over him, as he wrapped an arm around the big man's waist and guided him to a chair. "How tall are you?"

"Six-two. Give or take." Tanner's answer was almost a moan. Clearly, he was still in pain.

"Maybe it's just because of the way we were standing. You seem so much taller than me." Tanner closed his eyes, his hands gripping the arms of the canvas seat.

"First things first," Park said, shaking out two capsules from a small bottle. He poured water into a coffee cup. "Take these, they'll help with the pain."

Tanner followed the directions, and Park thought it might be a testament to just how much pain the man was in that he didn't bother to question the drugs. After all, they were total strangers.

Tanner's lids raised and deep brown eyes stared at him, as if trying to discern Park's nature. "I guess that was pretty stupid. You could've given me anything."

"I could have, but I didn't." He tugged on his ponytail and smiled at Tanner. "Hello, genuine hippie vegan-type here. I'm only going to give you things that are good for you. Okay, maybe that's not exactly true, but you won't find me pulling out a bottle of over-the-counter meds and handing out pieces like candy." He took the empty cup from Tanner and set it down on one of the stones surrounding the fire ring. Let's get you cleaned up, then you can crawl inside and go to bed." While he dipped a washcloth in warm water, Tanner looked over at the dark green nylon shelter.

"Pretty good-sized tent." Tanner hissed as the cloth was pressed against the side of his face.

"Have you seen my dog?" Park continued to swab then rinse until the cloth came away clean. "The edges are closing. This should have been cleaned sooner. When did you say this happened?"

"I don't really know. What day is this?" Tanner studied his face, as if searching for something beyond Park's words. He patted at his waistline. "Do I still have my cell phone?"

"Today is Monday. Your phone is dead, so there's no way to tell if it still works. I found you about nine this morning, it's now close to five." He wasn't providing any particularly useful information, but by talking he hoped to distract Tanner as he continued to work on his injury. It might have been taking a little bit of advantage of the situation when he started to wipe the other side of the man's face, but he justified it with the knowledge that Tanner was too hurt and too tired to take care of it himself. He would sleep better having some of the grime off his face and neck. Tanner lifted his chin and allowed Park to clean his neck as well. The moment stretched out, strangely intimate for two strangers who didn't even know each other's last name. It wasn't as if it was a hookup of any sort.

Tanner appeared to be as straight as they came, never once letting his gaze drop to any part of Park's body. No long looks, no flirty dialogue. Not a hint of an erection in sight. Damn the bad luck. If he was going to be in a tent, stuck in the middle of nowhere with a hunky stranger, couldn't the Fates have let him be gay? Wicked bitches.

"All right, big guy. We are all done here. Give me a minute to wash out this pot and then I'll get dinner. Okay?"

Tanner closed his eyes and nodded. "Just gonna sit here a little longer, then I'll get up to help."

"Like hell you will. You can help tomorrow if you're feeling better. Tonight we are going to see how the food stays down and make sure you get some sleep."

Tanner nodded slightly but a few minutes later his breathing returned to the slow steady rhythm it had been earlier when he was napping and Park wondered how much of his last comment had even been heard.

Humming slightly, Park started dinner then continued to move around the campsite. He added another log to the fire, put the sleeping bag inside the tent, and fed the dogs. With his hands on his hips, Park surveyed his surroundings. Once dinner was cleaned up and the trash stowed, there wouldn't be anything to attract any wild animals. The fire was safe and could burn down naturally, and there was enough firewood to stave off the morning chill. Finally satisfied everything was in order, he turned to Tanner, only to find him awake and watching.

"Why are you doing this?" Tanner asked.

Without answering right away, Park moved to the pot simmering on the camp stove and scooped more than half of the contents into a bowl and brought it to Tanner. "I hope you like chili." He handed the bowl over. "And by doing this... Do you mean making dinner? Because that's a no-brainer. I'm hungry."

Park moved back to the stove and served himself before sitting in the second camp chair.

Tanner continued to study him. "I mean, why are you taking care of me? I'm a total stranger and you have no idea how I came to be here. I could be a serial killer for all you know."

"Could you? That would be pretty damned interesting—I'd definitely have some questions for you." He returned Tanner's look with a smile.

"Now eat up, and since you're finally awake, you can tell me about yourself. Where you live, what's your sign, who's your girlfriend—you know, all the basic get-to-know-you chat between conscious adults."

He really hoped Tanner would let the conversation drop, because Park was certain he didn't want to explain the thoughts that were running through his mind. Mamma Sunshine would have a field day when he told her about this.

Tanner shook his head, but took a bite of the chili. "Mmm…good. Now answer the question. Why are you helping me?"

With a sigh, Park realized Tanner might just be a reincarnated bulldog chasing after a bone. He almost smiled at that image. Tanner took another bite, but continued to watch him steadily. *Great.* He finally found a man with endless patience and a one-track mind. A straight man. Sometimes life just wasn't fair. What had he done to deserve this?

"Honey, there was never a choice. Look around. You were hurt out in this vast wilderness, hundreds of miles from anywhere. I went left instead of right, passed two roads, but took the third. Scooby had to pee and instead found you... Pick your flavor. All I know is somewhere in the big bad world of destiny and fate, the planets and stars aligned, kismet turned a cartwheel, and the house of the rising sun flowed through Aquarius to let the sunshine in."

Tanner started to laugh. "I have no fucking idea what that means, but I think I like it."

****

Tanner ate his dinner without further comment, but continued to study Park surreptitiously. His long hair was still pulled back into a braid, emphasizing his high cheekbones and wide eyes. Really, men just weren't supposed to be that... Veering away from inappropriate thoughts about his rescuer, he focused on Park's comment about fate. It had made him laugh. However, now he was left wondering just exactly what the man meant. In terms of the overall scheme of the world, it did seem pretty incredible that Park managed to find him.

Not that Park had been looking, because as far as he knew only one or maybe two people on the planet actually knew Tanner was missing. Definitely the man who'd left him here to die. The question was what to do about the growing certainty that the man wielding the bat was none other than Tim—his own brother?

If T-bone had hit him, the intent had been deadly and he would no doubt return to make sure he'd finished the job. Tanner didn't remember much about the last…two days? But given what Park had said earlier about the scratches and the trail he'd made, it appeared as if some sense of self-preservation had guided him away from the site of the original attack. The characteristics of a chaparral landscape included rough sandy terrain that would show a clear path directly to this spot.

"Do you have a gun?" He hadn't intended to speak his thought out loud. Park's delicately arched brows rose, a look of surprise flashing across his face, signaling it wasn't a welcome question.

"Uh…that would be a big fat no, Rambo. Make love, not war and all that, you know?" Park said, the easy smile back in place.

"Why do you call me that? Rambo? And what kind of name is Park, anyway? Is it short for Parker?"

With a little laugh, Park nodded. "Yeah, people always ask that." He pointed to his chest. "I was conceived while my parents were traveling through the west, visiting national parks. Sunshine…that's my mom…wanted to name me Dakota, after Mount Rushmore. Dad wanted to call me Rocky after the mountains. Since I was born just outside Yellowstone, and they didn't like that as a name—thank the stars— they compromised on Park. Park Williams at your service."

Tanner stared at the smiling man for a moment, envious of the obviously oft-repeated happy family story. Then he shook his head, remembering the unanswered question. "And Rambo? Why do you call me that?" he repeated.

Park's smile faded a little and he shrugged. "You're wearing hunting gear. I assume you lost your own gun, and now you're asking about mine? I don't even eat meat—so no—hunting is not on my list of favorite things to do."

Unaccountably stung, Tanner wanted to protest. He didn't hunt either, although he couldn't deny eating meat. Instead, he tried to turn the focus on the other man. "How in the world did a vegetarian like you end up out here in Arizona cattle country?"

"Not vegetarian—vegan."

Tanner blinked. "There's a difference?"

"Just a bit. Why don't you tell me what *you* were doing out here. Maybe that will help us figure out how you got hurt."

Clearly the man had a one-track mind, and now that Tanner had opened the door to personal conversation, Park was like a dog with a bone. How could he explain the camouflage gear he was wearing? It was hard to argue with Park's logic since he *had* been hunting when he'd been injured. Shame burned through him as the memory returned. He'd been lying in wait to ambush the first rider he saw from the WSR. It didn't matter that he'd changed his mind at the last minute. The intention to hurt another had been there. The thought left him ill. He lowered his bowl of chili and turned away.

"Oh, hey. I'm sorry," Park said. "Here, let me take your bowl." Park was up and moving before Tanner could protest. Once he'd set their food aside, he returned with a flashlight and the first-aid kit. "Stay still for just a minute, I want to look at this once more. Do you always sleep on your side?"

"What? Uh…yes. I think so. Why?"

"I'm going to put a light gauze over the wound so you don't ooze."

Tanner stayed frozen in position, struck by the intimacy of the moment. Earlier, he'd either been too hurt or too weak to notice. Now, Park stood close, his crotch practically in Tanner's face. He hummed while he worked, the sound vibrating through Tanner, going straight to parts that needed to stay quiet. To stay down.

Park moved to stand between Tanner's knees and applied a salve to the wound. Tanner tried to pretend he didn't notice the taut denim hiding the cock obviously straining for attention. It was all he could do to keep from reaching out to touch the enticing bulge. *Shit.*

"Are you gay?" Tanner asked. Tension had caused his voice to come out more like a bark than he'd intended.

"Sweetheart," Park said and tilted Tanner's chin up with one finger. "If you have to ask, then I'm doing something wrong. But don't worry, I don't do straight boys. Your virtue is safe with me."

"I didn't—what I mean is—"

Finished with what he was doing, Park took half a step back and laughed. "You're kind of cute when you get flustered. Come on, it's bedtime for you. I hope you don't mind, but the four of us are going to share," Park said. He smiled in the direction of Scooby and Taco who were curled together on the far side of the fire. "Technically, the second sleeping bag is theirs."

"I'm sorry. Should I—" Tanner stood, then realized just how close together they were. He looked down into the beautiful face and got lost for a long moment in blue-gray eyes that seemed to see straight into his soul. Too bad his soul was so scarred. He shook off any misplaced attraction and took half a step back only to bump into his chair.

"You aren't going anywhere except to bed. I promise to keep to my side of the sleeping bag."

"How do you know I won't hurt you? I could be anybody."

"Funny. As if I could be anywhere else. I thought we established that earlier. For some reason still unfathomable to us, the universe decided we needed each other for a while. I suppose the passing goddesses could've decided to bring me out here just so you could kill me. That seems like a bit too much drama. I think I'll take my chances. Go into the tent and go to sleep, Tanner. The dogs can lay between us; I promise you're safe."

Chapter Three

Cass spread the scale drawing of the entire ranch over the table in his office. With his finger, he poked at the red X that marked the eastern-most boundary of the WSR. After a moment, he reached for his pencil and drew a crosshatch to indicate the last place the fence had been cut. He glanced over at the other two men and gave a long look.

"Ty, you know damn well I think you're capable—no hold that thought," he said as Ty looked like he was ready to interrupt him. "You're more than capable, without a doubt. I know you thought in the past that I didn't respect your ability. You're in this room with me and Chance because you're the most qualified person on the entire ranch when it comes to tactics and strategy."

He stood, stretching to his full height. "I don't know how much more of the sabotage we can take. Every time we think we have a handle on it, something new happens. This latest attack on Jesse was the final straw. Whoever is attacking our ranch made a mistake when he went after one of our people. I can deal with the down fence. Hell, I could even deal with the burned vacant bunkhouse. But what I won't fucking tolerate is somebody hurting one of my people. So the three of us are here, because Tyler, you know tactics. Chance, you know the law and you know how to circumvent it. And I know my ranch and I goddamn well know cowboys."

Ty sat back in the chair he'd straddled at the edge of the worktable and looked back, his face impassive. Across from him, Chance Carter chewed his lip and looked suspiciously like he might be trying to hide a laugh. Cass didn't care. He was pissed and this bullshit *would* stop.

"Are you both in? Because before we make any further plans, I want to know if either of you is going to hesitate when it comes to doing what's necessary to protect the people who live here."

Chance's smile was wide and his deep blue eyes seemed to sparkle with either mischief or satisfaction. Hell, probably with both. The man never had fit between the law enforcement lines. He was gonna make a damn fine cowboy after a few years of living out here on the ranch.

"I got you covered, boss. I just want to know what Holden knows about this. Because I don't want to put him in a compromising position," Chance said.

Cass nodded. It was a fine point. Holden was the former sheriff who had been gravely injured protecting Tyler and Cass. He'd temporarily lost the use of his legs and still walked with a cane. He would never be an official part of the law enforcement community again and yet he still had that fundamental belief in law and order. His suggestions tended to fall somewhere between calling the cops and building a bigger fence.

What Cass had in mind probably wouldn't fit within Holden's more traditional view of protection. "Holden does not need to know the particulars of our plan. He's well aware of who I chose to develop this strategy. He's not going to ask any questions he doesn't want the answers to. He'll stand by to step in when asked and we have his full support. Just don't tell him anything he doesn't need to hear. Clear?"

"Got it. I think I might like this assignment," Chance said with a chuckle.

Cass looked over at his lover. Tyler Harden. His soul mate if one believed in those sorts of things. And Cass had good mind to say he did believe. Well, at least he did now that Ty was in his life. The man's face was inscrutable, his light blue eyes hooded under heavy lids. He studied Cass as if he was either weighing what he wanted to say or trying to figure out some deeper meaning behind the words. "Ty, baby. Trust me, I need you with me on this."

Ty's smile was slow and just a little bit scary. "I got your back, cowboy. No place I'd rather be."

"Good, I just made the last mark on the map to show all of the places the property's been breached. I know both of you have heard this in bits and pieces from the various meetings we've had but let me just summarize for my own sake, if no one else's. Over the past several months, the WSR has been subject to several acts of sabotage. Remote fence lines cut and cattle turned loose. The bunkhouse right here in the compound burned down, and then finally escalating to the attack on Jesse."

"You know, Cass," Tyler said. "It's almost like there are two different hands at work. When you look at the location of the downed fences, there is no doubt that creating havoc and letting the livestock loose was part of the plan, but it could have been much worse had he picked one of these paddocks." Tyler pointed to the grazing spots closer to the ranch house where the Angus were fed.

"Same thing with the bunkhouse. As much as it fucking sucked, that fire could have been catastrophic. When you consider all of the buildings in the main ranch compound–especially the four occupied bunkhouses, three occupied casitas, and the main ranch house. The message by picking a residence was far more threatening than picking a storage shed, for example, but still was designed not to hurt anyone."

"I agree," Chance said.

Cass nodded. "It's no secret to any of us here that I believe the Trip-T is behind our trouble. I have to wonder if maybe the left hand doesn't know what the right hand is doing. But by going after one of our people, I can't help believe the game has changed.

The question is how do we prove it and what are we gonna do about it?"

"How much money do you want to put behind this?" Tyler asked.

"What are you thinking?"

I think we need to know more, but given the thousands of acres and miles of fence lines involved, there's no way we can monitor everything. We sure as hell can't hire enough ranch hands to cover it all," Ty said.

"Agreed," Cass said.

"I think putting up a few surveillance cameras makes good sense. I know," Ty continued, raising his hand as if to stop any protests. "That's a bit extreme for the type of business you do out here. But now were talking physical security. Some well-placed cameras in the areas that strategically lend themselves to egress makes the most sense, because the first order of business, beyond the immediate safety of everyone concerned, is identification of the bastard who has us in his sights."

"All right. This is more in your field of expertise, so the two of you mark on this map where we want to set up cameras. Is this something we need to hire someone for or do we have the capability to do it ourselves?"

"Hire someone," Chance said. "I know where we can go for that information. I'll take that on and bring you a quote."

"I'm not overly concerned with the cost, Chance, but we need it goddamn quick. What else, Ty?"

"Here's where you have to make a choice, Cass. Generally, you don't want your target to think you suspect anything. So either you continue to put your people out there and hope no one's gunning for them or you risk telegraphing your suspicions. Since we've already made changes around the ranch based on the previous incidents, I don't think it would come as any surprise if we changed a few of our procedures, but if we pull back and stop all activity outside the main compound, I think were sending the wrong signal.

"I suggest we still do patrols but everybody works in pairs and they vest up. We'll probably never know for sure what happened to Jesse, but it would've been a hell of a lot harder to get at him if he'd been riding with someone else. They are targeting singles for now. Keep everything else in place—or maybe work a little closer to the main compound, but not overly so."

"All right. Done. Anything else?" Cass asked as he pulled his lip and stared at the map.

"Yes, boss," Chance said. "You don't own this. If this is the work of the Trip-T or for that matter any homegrown militia or so-called freedom fighters, then this is domestic terrorism. Plain and simple. I think this is more work by whoever was behind killing those feds and taking Bryan." He paused for a moment, his handsome face drawn into sharp angles.

"I know the locals are still trying to pass off that Willie Hutchinson masterminded that kidnapping and was acting alone. I call bullshit. I studied the man and there is nothing… *Nothing* to indicate he had the skills or the resources necessary to pull off the kidnapping of two federal agents by himself. The place he was living was practically a shack, yet he drove a late model truck, owned a few weapons, plus the four-wheeler. His only visible means of support was leasing a few grazing acres. He was attached to somebody somewhere—he had to be.

"Now that I'm on the outside, I can't quite get that information so easily, but I will. Meanwhile, do you remember when Ty and I went after Bryan? There was a piece of shit shack about ten miles away from Hutchinson's place. It got overlooked in the final investigation because everyone zeroed in on the location of the murders. I'd like to check it out."

Chance looked across the table. "What you say, Ty? You up for a little field trip tonight?"

****

T-bone stood quietly outside the family room, listening for a long minute to make sure the room was empty before he pushed his way inside. Not that he was avoiding his father. *Not exactly*. It would just be better if he could manage to get out of the house without any questions asked. There was a piece of garbage he'd left out there on the WSR and it was time to go find Tanner and make sure he never came home again. He'd spent all weekend waiting for the cops to show up to notify his father of Tanner's death and of the damage his brother had done to the WSR cowboy. It was how the scene had been set to appear and the scenario should have played out by now—but he'd started to get nervous without any news of Tanner's fate.

Fortunately, the ranch hands coming back from Kingman after the weekend were full of news about the happenings at the neighboring ranch. It seemed that the rodeo cowboy, Jesse Duran, had been the one who was hurt in the staged accident. It should have looked as if Tanner and the other cowboy had been in a fight, but maybe since Duran was a guest and relatively famous, Cartwright had decided to search sooner rather than later. Whatever. All he knew was the cowboy gossip network said Duran had been injured, didn't remember the attack, and no one mentioned anyone else involved in the incident.

The plan had evolved on the spot, but there shouldn't have been any doubt about what had happened to Tanner. His attention had been focused on surrendering to the approaching rider and it had been easy to move in fast, the bat already swinging at his brother's head, even as he'd turned slightly at the last second. The contact had jarred his elbow and left his wrist stinging but the boneless manner in which his brother landed on the ground had been proof enough he wouldn't be walking away.

After dirtying himself up, T-bone had gotten into position and called for help as soon as the approaching rider was close enough. From there, it had been a simple matter to drop a rock on top of the other man and leave him for dead. The injuries were severe enough that both men should have succumbed to the elements or the scavengers. He hadn't really given a shit which came first.

So why hadn't anyone found Tanner when they'd found Duran? He supposed there was a miniscule possibility that Tanner had been discovered and carted out to the Willow Springs, but T-bone didn't believe that. That was too big a secret for ranch hands to keep on a Saturday night when beer was a buck a bottle at the Cow Poke in Kingman.

Stepping inside, he made his way to the light weapons cabinet. They had plenty of heavy firepower stored more securely on the Trip-T, but this particular mission—as he liked to think of them—needed to look like a cowboy out surveying his land. It would come as a total shock when he discovered his oldest brother many days dead and little more than carrion feed.

With his own .45 he always carried hanging heavy on his hips, all he planned to take was a rifle. The knife in his boot rounded out everything he'd need.

"Going somewhere, Tim?"

"Shit. I didn't hear you come in, Dad."

"No, I expect given the amount of time you stood outside this door to make sure the room was empty, my walking in here and finding you is quite a surprise. What are you up to, Son?" his father asked again.

"I ain't up to nothing. I'm going out to ride the perimeter. With Tanner gone, someone has got to keep an eye on the outlying rangeland. You hear anything from him yet?"

"Funny, I was just getting ready to ask you the same thing. On the other hand, sometimes there are things I don't need to know. I'm counting on you now, Timothy. So is the general. We both realize it's going to take more than a couple of downed fences to get those perverts off the Willow Springs. I truly believe that what they do out there is an abomination to the Lord. I know you see things my way, Son. Tanner—well, let's just say I believe he might be misguided in his thinking."

The old man walked to the drink cart and idly fingered the decanter holding his favorite whiskey. T-bone wondered if his dad was going to openly start drinking this early in the morning, and with a mental shrug, he realized it didn't really matter. Before the year was out, T-bone planned to be the sole owner of the Trip-T. Let the rumors start circulating now that old man Trip drank himself into a grave upon hearing the news of his oldest son's death.

Locking the gun cabinet and setting the key on top of the custom wooden case, he turned and faced his father.

"Dad, I'm not going to get between anything with you and Tanner. If you have problems with him, you need to talk them out. All I know is there's a hell of a lot of work here with only one of us riding range and giving orders to the ranch hands. Either Tanner needs to get back to work or Thomas needs to come back from Flagstaff. Meanwhile I got shit to do. I might be out of cell range for a while, but if you need something, text me. I gotta go now so I can get back, because there's a lot of shit to do back here too."

He felt his father's gaze on his back as he stormed through the door. It didn't matter. Dad would be drunk in a matter of hours, the whole conversation likely forgotten.

The kitchen was quiet as T-bone made his way through and grabbed his hat before heading out the back door. With a scowl on his face and no bullshit about his walk, he blew past the ranch foreman and headed straight for the vehicle barn. Once inside, he selected one of their four-wheelers and stowed his rifle. The engine turned over smoothly, the noise bouncing off the corrugated steel walls as he fired his way outside. Without a word to anyone, T-bone headed west, anxious to get this discovery over with.

*

Hours later, T-bone wasn't any better informed about his brother's location. Tanner's truck was right where he'd left it, pulled off the fire road and hidden from the casual passers-by. He'd hiked the same trail as the other day, and it was clear from the boot prints in the sandy soil that other than the two of them, no one else had passed by. He had a regular mystery on his hands.

It hadn't been hard to follow the trail down below the ridge where he'd left his brother, either. Hoof and shoe prints told the story of how they'd gotten Duran out of there. But nothing indicated the WSR rescue party had climbed the cliff or had even looked around once they'd found Jesse.

Where the fuck was Tanner? Considering all the likely scenarios, the one that brought the most dread was the idea that Tanner was even now recovering on the Willow Springs Ranch. If Cass Cartwright had Tanner, they were in big trouble. The last thing the big cowboy needed was proof that the Trip-T was behind the attacks on his ranch.

Pushing his hat back on his head, T-bone climbed back on the quad to continue his search.

Chapter Four

Tanner was in big trouble. Not the your-brother-is-a-sociopathic-murderer-and-you're-his-next-victim sort of trouble. Not even the your-father-is-trying-to-overthrow-the-federal-government-and-you're-going-to-jail-for-helping kind of trouble. No…this was the sort of trouble that came when you woke up with your arm draped over another man's waist and your dick pressed against his ass. Holy fuck. How was he going to get out of this?

He'd been facing the outer wall of the tent with Taco pressed against his back last night when Park had made his way inside. Exhausted and injured, Tanner had fallen asleep within minutes. Sometime in the night, he and the big dog had swapped places, and there was no room for him to pull back from his position pressed against Park's back.

To be honest, there wasn't a single part of him that wanted to put space between them. Park's long blond hair was loose and Tanner's face was buried in the soft strands. The man smelled good. No, better than good. Like evergreens and fresh air, a hint of smoke from the campfire. Like being outside. It just felt right to have his cock pressed against the man's ass, his arm wrapped around the slender waist. And everything about that was wrong.

Not wrong in the way his homophobic father would have said. No…Tanner had come to terms years ago with the knowledge he was gay. He could even say it in his head now without wincing—but other than visiting a few porn sites, he hadn't actually done anything involving another man. Now, thoughts of doing—everything—displayed on his mental drive-in theater. And that just simply couldn't happen. It really didn't matter how many reasons he came up with to explain why this was a bad idea, only one was important. If T-bone or any of his father's men found out Tanner was gay, he'd be dead, and they wouldn't hesitate to take Park out, too.

They would kill Park. They would kill Tanner. He repeated those words in his head and wondered at a world where that type of hate and fear made sense. Not just any world. *His world*. His brother—his own father. *Jesus Christ*. He was lying in a tent, his hand on a stranger's dick, and only now understood the true depth of his family's sins. Of his own shame.

"Hey, don't stop on my account, honey," said a sleepy voice as Park pushed back against Tanner, his hips rocking into the impromptu hand job. "Nice way to wake up. Didn't think this was your style…"

Behind him, Taco stretched, forcing him even closer to Park, who moaned at the contact.

Tanner ordered his hand to let go but other parts of his brain seemed pretty content to hold on. And stroke. Oh God…was that him making those sounds low in his throat? His own cock was hard enough to pound nails and leaking all over Park's ass. Just the thought of slicking them both up and sliding his dick into—

The far off sound of a quad engine ripped him from both the fantasy and the reality faster than full immersion in an ice bath. In one motion, he jerked his hand back and threw the sleeping bag off both of them.

"Hold on, Tanner. It's okay, lots of guys are curious—" Park said, reaching for the warmth of their cover.

"Get up," Tanner hissed. "Jesus Christ, get the fuck up and get dressed. We've got to get out of here. Will your dogs run or stay with you?"

Blinking rapidly, Park seemed to catch some of Tanner's urgency and began to pat around the tent, reaching for his clothes. "Uhm, Scooby might run off, Taco will stay. I don't—"

"No time. Someone is looking for us." He shook his head. "For me," he amended. "We've got to go, now. Grab Scooby and don't let go. Tell me what you need to have with you and I'll carry as much as I can. We'll come back for the other stuff later. Jesus, Park, hurry. They'll kill us." Tanner thrust one foot into his jeans, his coordination shot from the ache in his muscles. Amidst the commotion, Taco lumbered to his feet, looking as shocked as a Great Dane was capable of looking. He shook his head, slobber flying, then started to circle, apparently deciding going back to sleep was better than all the jumping around. Scooby stood in the corner of the tent, his front legs stiff, tail and hackles raised. Tanner lurched sideways, trying to hold onto the top of the tent for support so he could lift his left foot high enough to step into his jeans.

At Tanner's movement, Scooby growled, then started an incessant yapping, his front paws bouncing with the effort. "Shut up, Scoob," Park said, sliding his jeans onto his legs, before standing and closing the zip. He tugged a shirt over his head, then looked at Tanner. "Man, are you sure? Because seriously, you've been really out of it. This is probably just some sort of reaction—"

"Look, we don't have time. I heard the four-wheeler. It might not be who I think— Let's not take a chance, okay? These are seriously fucked up people, and they will be looking for me. I never should have let you help."

Park snorted, but Tanner was pleased to see he was lacing his boots.

"I'm sorry. Just help me get us out of here this morning. I'll come back and get your stuff, I promise. Please, Park?"

Grabbing Scooby up into one arm, like he was carrying a football, Park nodded, his blond hair flying around his face. "Let's go back to Kingman and get some Starbucks."

"I've got a better idea. How do you feel about visiting a real working ranch?"

****

Park wasn't usually someone at a loss for words, but Tanner honestly confused the hell out of him. They'd been driving nearly forty-five minutes and he'd been unable to get more than a word or two in response to his open-ended questions. *Tell me about your family…*

"Nothing to say."

Do you remember more about your injuries?

"Not really."

Can you tell me where we're going?

"Willow Springs Ranch."

That last answer had stopped Park's questions and started his mind churning. He knew much more about the WSR than Tanner would have suspected. What he knew had his mind working overdrive trying to sort out who exactly had a hand on Park's dick this morning.

In his previous life—okay, only a few days ago—Park had been gainfully employed by the CPS, investigating child abuse. He'd learned a lot about the west Arizona ranch when Chad Ollom, a former Flagstaff substitute teacher was falsely accused of abuse. Considering Chad had been living and working more than three hours away at the WSR for nearly a year, the timing of the claim was the first thing that made Park suspicious. It turned out the whole thing was a set up, and the father who filed the claim should have been brought up on charges.

In his opinion, the false claims were no doubt related to the fact Chad was gay—but the county attorney hadn't seen things Park's way. The best Park could do was to warn Chad and his lover that someone seemed to be framing him—talk about sounding melodramatic.

At any rate, Park had become quite interested in the WSR, which was what led him west, to the lower elevations and the pinyon-juniper landscape of Mohave County. From what he could gather, WSR owner Cass Cartwright was a city boy turned rancher and some kind of fairy godfather to a bunch of gay cowboys. This little impromptu trip would let him catch up with Chad and maybe get the whole story about the ranch.

Like…what was Tanner's connection to a bunch of gay cowboys? Because despite the straight first impression, nothing screamed gay like your hand wrapped around another guy's cock.

"It's about another mile up ahead," Tanner said. His voice came out strained.

Glancing over at his passenger, Park took in the tight-fingered grip on the door, the clenched jaw, the nearly rigid line of his posture.

"Something wrong, honey?"

"Nothing that needs to worry you."

"Ouch," Park said. "Just so long as you aren't leading me into a trap with whoever beat you…"

Tanner half-coughed, half-laughed, but none of it sounded happy. He sighed and with a visible effort, leaned back and relaxed into his seat. "I might be walking into what's considered enemy territory. You'll be safe enough if you wait in the van until after I get out. I'll make sure they know you're not really with me, okay?"

"Are you going to be in some kind of danger? Was it someone at the WSR who hurt you?"

Tanner snorted, but didn't answer as the van rumbled over the metal cattle guard. "Pull up over there," he said, pointing to a long, low adobe-style ranch house.

After miles of dirt road, they'd ended up in a fenced compound of ranch buildings. A barn with several pickup trucks parked out front dominated one end, flanked by some other nondescript outbuildings. He bumped past some small houses and pulled to a stop in front of the main house.

A tall man in jeans, boots, a cowboy hat, and holster stepped from the door, smiling in their direction. Then his gaze shifted and fixed on the passenger side of the van, his ready smile fading fast. He turned his head slightly, shouted something over his shoulder, then moved from the doorway to cover half the distance to their vehicle before he stopped.

He stood in the shade, his expression grim, hands hanging loose by his sides. *Shit.* He didn't look as though he was messing around. The next few minutes could be a lot more dangerous than Park had anticipated.

Even as he shifted the van into park, he reached to put a hand on Tanner's arm. "Wait. There's another guy at the door over there," he said and pointed to the far end of the house. Something in the other man's hand flashed silver in the sunlight. A knife? Crap.

"Tanner, I don't like this at all. Oh damn…" he said, looking over at the barn. At least six other men had stepped outside, all of them looking in their direction. All of them wearing guns. Tanner's fingers twitched on the door handle and Park tightened his grip. "Tombstone is supposed to be south of here, isn't it?" he asked and wished it was more of a joke.

"Yeah. Look, I appreciate everything you've done, but maybe it would be better if you left as soon as I get out of the van, okay?"

"I don't think so. In fact, maybe we should—" He gripped the gear shift, prepared to put it in reverse. One of the men from the barn broke free of the group and started loping toward him, waving his hands at the others. Park stared, trying to see past the hat and wild arm motions. Something about him seemed…

From the backseat, Scooby's growl triggered the memory. The tangle of leashes, collars, and dogs as

Scooby broke free and ran straight for the traffic on a busy Route 66 in Flagstaff. Jesse Duran making a frantic dive and catching the Chihuahua-shaped bullet as he sped past. No doubt his orange and white van was memorable enough that Jesse recognized him. Hopefully, the man could calm things down long enough for Park and Tanner to get out of this in one piece. Although it was hard to say what the tension was over, since his new…friend was disinclined to explain any damn thing.

Like watching a pantomime, the two of them sat locked inside the van while Jesse made his way to stand directly in front of them, his hands held up in a gesture of peace as he faced the big cowboy in front of the house.

"Tanner? Do you know who is who around here?"

"The only one who matters is the one who came out of the front door. That's Cartwright, and he's the one I need to talk to." He pulled up on the lever and the latch sounded loud as he opened the van door, but before he pushed it all the way open, Tanner turned and stared at Park. His face was pale under the bruises and his mouth was a tight, thin line as he studied Park's face.

"Thank you. You didn't even know me, yet you helped. You saved my life and I've repaid that by bringing you into a dangerous situation. For that— and so much more—I'm truly sorry. Please, Park, as soon as I'm out of the van, drive away and don't look back. There isn't anything that's going to happen to me here that I don't deserve. You and Scooby and Taco… Be safe."

Before Park could say a word, Tanner jumped from the van and slammed the door. Cartwright drew his gun and with a steady hand, took aim.

Park opened his door and climbed out, unsure of his own intentions, but he wasn't about to let anyone shoot Tanner, who stood with his hands raised in a universal gesture of surrender.

"Goddammit, Cass," Jesse shouted. "Hang on a fucking minute."

The pint-size growl from the back of the van turned into a steady yap as Scooby jumped through the open door and passed by him in a flash to run straight toward Cartwright. Taco lumbered out, and jumped to the ground with an inelegant thud, then loped to Tanner's side. The normally placid dog's hackles were raised and his growl came from deep in his chest. One hundred seventy-five pounds of pissed off Great Dane was impressive.

"You armed, Triplett?" Cass shouted.

"No, sir." Tanner's response was soft, but carried clearly despite the accompanying chorus of dog barks.

"I'll check him for weapons," said a deep voice from behind him. Park had been so caught up in the drama unfolding before him he hadn't even noticed the large black man who had approached from the other side of the van.

"Lace your fingers on the back of your head, Tanner. Spread your legs and don't move." Despite the blue jeans, cowboy boots, and cane, the way the man moved spoke of law enforcement. After a thorough and very professional-looking pat down, he stepped back. "He's unarmed."

Tanner kept his hands behind his head. "I need to talk with you, Cass."

"Did your father send you?"

"My father…" Tanner turned his head toward Park. Their gazes met and held a long moment before a shudder shook Tanner's broad shoulders. He turned to face Cass once again. "Several days ago, my father sent me to ambush and kill one of your men. Park and his dogs, here"—he smiled quickly down at Taco— "don't know anything about this. He just gave me a ride. If you'll let them leave, I'll tell you everything that's happening at the Trip-T."

Just what in the hell was going on around here? Total chaos—that was what. There were people with guns and his tiny Chihuahua might be on the verge of a stroke. At Tanner's words, a chorus of curses carried across the yard and Taco added his own big booming bark to the cacophony.

Park blinked. He really should check his horoscope—there had to be something in the stars to explain all this. Fate had led him to a man who was maybe a killer and stupid enough to think he could dismiss Park as nothing more than a taxi. As if there was a chance in hell Park would just up and drive away without the whole story.

"Oh, I'm not going anywhere just yet…"

Chapter Five

The main house at the WSR was strangely similar to his house at the Trip-T. Well, maybe not all that strange, given the remote locations and practical homebuilding for the extreme summer heat and cold winters. The house was a southwestern adobe-style, with low, wood beam ceilings, arched doorways, and tinted windows. Cass led the way to a large, comfortable-looking great room, filled with dark woods and bright throws. A couple of authentic-looking Navajo rugs hung on the walls, while some less expensive and far more practical replicas decorated the floor.

Tanner took the seat near the fireplace, leaving his back to the wall, and a platoon of Cartwright's men between him and the only exit. At least he could be grateful it wasn't everyone on the ranch. Cass had sent most of the men back to work, but still facing this band of older and more experienced men wasn't going to be easy. Good thing he'd had these last couple of years to practice hiding his thoughts, as well as his nerves.

While everyone else took their time settling into spots around the room, Tanner studied each man. Tyler Hardin, Cass's lover, leaned against the doorway, his big forearms crossed over his chest, his gaze locked on Tanner. Rumors about the man had him as a former Navy SEAL with serious injuries left over from a few tours in Afghanistan.

Only slightly less intense, the former sheriff, Holden Titus, leaned on his cane near the window, his eyes scanning the room before returning repeatedly back to Tanner. A tall man with black hair and blue eyes sat on one of the long couches and crossed one ankle over the other knee. His face gave nothing away, but there was something about the man that telegraphed cop. The former rodeo star Jesse Duran flopped on the other sofa, glancing at Tanner and then turning to look steadily at the last man in the room. The last man Tanner wanted there. Park Williams.

"There's really no need for Park to hear any of this." Tanner tried again to have his rescuer leave the room before he revealed the plot against Cass Cartwright and the men of the Willow Springs Ranch. Especially before he got to the part about his own role in the sabotage. His stomach began to churn and Tanner hoped he wouldn't throw up before he finished this confession.

"Cass, Park here is the social worker from Child Protective Services who cleared Chad's name. I'm not exactly certain how—or if—this all ties together but I think we should have him stay," Jesse said.

"I have the people in this room I want here, for now," Cass said. He moved to sit on the couch. "I'm going to assume you know who everyone is…"

Dropping his foot to the ground, the black-haired stranger leaned forward, a casual smile on his face. "I don't believe I've ever had the privilege of meeting this young man. Chance Carter." His smile broadened, the lines around his eyes showed it was an expression the man must wear often.

"Tanner Triplett," he responded and tentatively smiled back, wondering if this man might prove to be a voice of reason once the truth was known.

"So I gathered. I hope you're not responsible for the trouble we've had around here. Particularly anything associated with the death of those feds or the kidnapping and attempted murder of one of our men. I'd really hate to have to kill you."

Ty snorted, but Park sucked in a quick breath and looked about to speak from his position next to Jesse on the other couch.

"Don't worry, Park." Tanner automatically sought to soothe his new and misguided acquaintance. "He's joking. But really, you should go."

"Am I?" Chance said coolly.

"Enough," Cass said. "You're safe enough for now, Tanner. However, I suggest you get talking and don't bother to try to hide anything or hold back information. You happen to be facing some of the best investigators in the state, and you have no idea how much information they already have about the Trip-T."

"Yes, sir." Tanner sat a little straighter in his chair and focused his attention directly on Cass. "You know my father doesn't own the Trip-T, right? When my grandfather passed a few years ago, he left it in trust to my brothers and me. My father has a lifetime interest, but can't sell it or make major changes to the property without the approval of the trustees—a bunch of lawyers in Flag, who have yet to approve anything he's requested. I don't know if that's what changed my father or if my grandfather already knew there was something wrong, but he's never been quite right since he found out. Oh hell, who am I kidding? He's been a frustrated bigot my entire life, but being passed over for the ranch made everything much worse.

"The fact is, he hooked up with some wannabe general who plans to make the whole Northeast corner of Arizona its own nation. No blacks, no Hispanics, and most definitely no gays."

There were several muttered curses, but Cass held up his hand for silence. "All right, how does the Willow Springs Ranch fit into this picture?"

"I knew the general was a right-wing extremist and had become increasingly influential in my father's life until everything became about the Armed Resistance

Militia—that's what they call themselves. The general and my father have started stockpiling weapons, building underground bunkers, and the plan is to start moving more of his men here next year sometime.

"At first, I thought my father would tire of his obsession with this separatist movement, but as he got sucked further in, so did I. Oh, not with their beliefs, but with the small jobs I was assigned to help the cause. I was just trying to placate my father, but each one seemed to ask for more, and I didn't know how to get out of it without losing my father and my ranch." He shook his head. "It was just so little at first." Tanner blew out a breath, but no one spoke. No one moved.

"A few days ago, my brother T-bone told me that the general wants the WSR as his headquarters and is threatening to pull his nation building to some land he has access to in Montana if my father can't deliver your land. I thought the attacks had to do with the three of them…my father, the general, and T-bone being homophobes and wanting their new nation"— he made air quotes—"free from gays. That's what they'd been saying.

"I told them they'd never chase you from this ranch, Cass, but they were determined. They are willing to do whatever it takes." Tanner stopped talking and waited for the inevitable questions. He couldn't look at Park, didn't want to see the disappointment on the other man's face. *Damn.* Maybe if he'd met someone like Park sooner…

Cass tugged at his lower lip for a minute before he finally spoke. "So we have the basic motivation behind the sabotage and it's more complex than just homophobia. Do we have the saboteur sitting here in the room with us or are you going to try to blame that all on your brother, too?"

"No, sir, I'm not. I mean I'm not going to blame it all on T-bone. Honestly, I don't know everything he's carried out on my father's orders but I do know some of it." He met Chance's cold blue stare. "T-bone was involved with the planned disruption of the wild horse gather by the BLM. There was a lot of closed-door meetings to which I wasn't invited." He shifted his gaze back to Cass. "But I'm not innocent, either. I'm the one responsible for cutting your fence and freeing your livestock. And—" Tanner looked down at the toes of his boots and prayed for a hole to open up and swallow him.

The room was silent as the others waited him out. When the earth failed to grant his request, he raised his head and swallowed hard. "I started the fire that burned down your new dorm."

Then he turned his head and looked straight at Jesse. "And God forgive me, but I was waiting out there under orders to kill the first WSR ranch hand who rode that trail. I recognized you through my field glasses, but honest to God, I wasn't going to shoot."

He frowned as jumbled memories of that day tried to sort themselves into words. "I was up on the ridge, watching you approach, when I decided enough was enough. I tied my white T-shirt to the barrel of my rifle but before I could raise it to draw your attention, something—someone—" He fingered the wound on the side of his head and looked toward the window. "I don't know what happened after that."

"I'll tell you what happened after that," Park said. "I admit my curiosity was piqued with Chad's story about the WSR and this area of Arizona. Since I was taking another installment of my retirement, I decided to bring my dogs to Mohave County for a little off-grid camping. You know the BLM land east of here is open for disbursed camping, right?"

At Cass's quick nod, Park glanced at Tanner, then continued. "That's where I was headed, and when I stopped to let the dogs out, Scooby took off. By the time I caught up, the dogs had found Tanner, badly beaten, dehydrated, and nearly dead." Park's mouth tightened into a thin line for a minute.

"Someone tried to kill him, probably for trying to wave you down," he said with a nod to Jesse. "Whoever hit Tanner, left him for dead, and given the temps and his condition, they should have succeeded. He refused medical treatment, so I set up a camp, cleaned his wound, and gave him some food and water. Early this morning, we heard the drone of a four-wheeler not far from where we'd camped. I think it's entirely possible whoever did this will try again if it's discovered Tanner is still alive."

Cass's mouth twitched, but Chance spoke first. "You've known him for what? Twelve hours, and you figured all that out from this conversation? For your information, Jesse was hurt three days ago. Are you trying to tell us he was out there that long without supplies?"

"Three days?" Tanner asked, completely confused by the passage of time. Was it even remotely possible he'd been out there that long? "I don't understand—"

Park spoke over Tanner. "I'm a trained observer, and pretty damned good at sizing up situations quickly. For example, *Chance,* we might have just met, but it didn't take me long to peg you as an asshole."

"Okay, everybody, hold on," Cass said as tempers flared once again. "Tanner, you've just confessed to destroying property, arson, and who knows what other charges could be filed." He held up his hand as Holden started to answer. "Rhetorical question…"

Cass stood. "I have some maps in my office. You come next door and show me the areas where you cut the fence and any places where you think there might be these bunkers you talked about. If we believe you, I'll give you two choices. You can stay here and work off some of your debt while we get this straightened out or you can go straight to jail. If we catch you lying—"

"Yes, sir. I mean I'll tell you everything I know. I won't lie. I know I can't make up for everything I've done, but you have my word that I'll do whatever I can."

"You can start by not calling me sir. Makes me feel old as shit."

"Nah," Ty said. "You are old as dirt, Cass. Where do you want to put Tanner? I don't think it would be a good idea to leave him in a bunkhouse unsupervised. How about the guest room?"

"You can put both of us in there," Park said, stepping over to put a hand on Tanner's shoulder.

Cass raised a brow.

Park spoke before anyone raised an objection. "You can't imagine that as an impartial observer listening to all of this, including Chance's threats, I would let this man stay here without at least one unbiased observer looking after his safety. For all I know, the only reason you're not calling the cops is so you can finish the job someone else already started."

"It's okay, Park. Really, you've done enough." He outweighed the beautiful man by a good thirty pounds, yet Park was standing there, thinking Tanner deserved to be protected against the anger of the men at the WSR. The men were armed, ranch-savvy cowboys, who could break Park in two, if they had a mind to, but everything from the set of his jaw to the way his slender shoulders squared up under the scrutiny of the others telegraphed the seriousness of Park's words. It was sexy as hell.

His fingers twitched at an unbidden, tactile memory of his hand wrapped around Park's cock. Oh hell no—so not sharing a room with the too sexy stranger. He could already imagine the kind of hell the Trip-T would rain down on the WSR just for Park being here. If they found out he was—well, he just couldn't let that happen.

"Are you sure that's a good idea, Tyler?" Holden asked. "You do realize that Old Man Trip will come after Tanner?" Holden said, as if giving voice to Tanner's thoughts.

Ty straightened from where he'd been leaning against the wall, watching the proceedings. "Yep— I'm counting on it. That's why I'm keeping him close to me. Come on, Tanner. Let me show you your room. You need a shower before we get all cozy around those maps."

Feeling like he was on a roller coaster straight to hell, Tanner stood and followed Ty and Park. In that sudden stillness that happens in a crowded room, Jesse's words followed him down the hall.

"You do realize that boy is as queer as I am, don't you?"

****

"Mother fuck," T-bone said as he kicked at the already upended camp chair, sending it skittering across the dirt to land on its side next to the fire pit. Tanner had help. This was seriously going to fuck things up.

Apparently, Tanner's head was a lot harder than he'd thought, because not only was there a bloody trail showing he'd survived the blow, now that T-bone had finally tracked his brother down, it was only to discover he'd arrived too late. A campsite showing all the signs of a hurried departure was the only thing remaining.

"Okay, T-bone. What are you going to do now? Did someone from the WSR find Tanner or was this a random meeting?"

It was too much of a coincidence to think that Tanner crawled all this way to find some total stranger to rescue him. They were right on the border of the Willow Springs—his brother had probably already been planning to meet up with one of them fuckin' queers. That would've been why he was raising the white flag rather than taking aim. Well, there wasn't much to do now, except go back and tell his father that Tanner had betrayed them and was now missing.

T-bone used the kindling and logs someone had gathered previously and started a fire. While the flames built, he dismantled the tent, searching through every pocket to ensure there was nothing giving away the owner's name or address—on the off chance Tanner wasn't at the WSR. Finding nothing, he tossed the tent onto the flames and watched as the nylon structure turned to a layer of plastic, black acrid smoke billowing up. The smoke from the fire would be seen for miles, but he didn't give a fuck. The flames would die down soon enough, and despite the always-present fire danger, a random smoke plume that disappeared quickly rarely caused concern. After adding the chairs and the sleeping bags, T-bone climbed onto his four-wheeler and headed back to give his father a version of events that was guaranteed to get Tanner out of the way, permanently.

*

"Timothy, good to see you, young man. I was just speaking with your father about some new plans. I believe I have some work for you," the general said.

"It's good to see you too, sir," T-bone said. Although he hadn't been expecting to see the general when he returned, he was not about to let this opportunity pass. "You know I'm willing to do whatever you need, sir, however, I wondered if I might be able to share some news with the two of you first. It's rather urgent."

"Certainly. What is it, Son?"

The irony of the general referring to him as Son was not lost on him, but T-bone turned to face his real father. "I'm afraid I have some news about Tanner that isn't going to make you very happy. I've suspected he was keeping secrets for a while but it's only been the last three days I've discovered the full depth of his betrayal. I've been doing a lot of searching around the borders of the WSR, examining their security, looking for weaknesses, tracking their patterns. I thought Tanner was doing the same, but now I think he may have a different relationship with one or more of the men at the Willow Springs Ranch."

Trip's hand shook as he listened to his son's words, as if he suspected what might be coming next. Hell, perhaps he did. It was pretty damned obvious that his older brother didn't date and had never seemed interested in anything other than the Trip-T.

"What are you saying? Has Tanner done something?" His father's voice came out in a harsh whisper.

"Tanner hasn't been seen for the last three days. Not since he was supposed to take care of that little bit of business on the WSR. This morning I found evidence he's been camping just over the fence line on Cartwright's land. I'm sorry, Dad, but he wasn't alone and we both know exactly what kind of men they are over there."

His father's face turned a nasty shade of gray and he collapsed onto the couch. "It can't be true. That boy was raised to know the difference between right and wrong."

"Now, Trip," the general said, facing T-bone's father. "God-fearing people like yourself raise their children right, but that doesn't mean Satan isn't waiting to steer them wrong. If Tanner has thrown his lot in with the homosexuals, then he deserves to have the fires of hell rise up around him. Timothy, how sure are you that Tanner is with one of Cartwright's men?"

T-bone looked down and pressed his lips tightly together while he slowly shook his head from side to side, as if upset by the news he was about to deliver.

Finally, he looked up and met his father's gaze. There were two sleeping bags in the tent, both unzipped and spread open, one on top of the other, like a bed. Both sides had been slept in and there was evidence of recent…sexual activity," T-bone lied. "The sleeping bags were labeled with the WSR brand. Tanner's watch and some of his clothing was piled in the corner along with another man's jeans. I don't think there can be any doubt, sir."

"That's a damned shame." The general moved to clap a heavy hand on T-bone's shoulder and turned to face the elder Triplett. "We're going to have to do something about this. That boy knows too much to risk him speaking out of school."

T-bone nodded, then added the final piece he hoped would push his father over the edge. "I couldn't find a name for which one of the queers he was with—but it's damned clear he's moved over to the WSR. I burned everything, as long as we find a way to contain the situation quickly, no one else will ever be able to prove Tanner was ever there. I just hope he doesn't tell them any of our plans."

Trip raked a shaky hand through his silver hair and looked toward the drink cart. "No, no, you're right. Tanner's sins are his own. I only thank the heavens that your dear mother isn't here to see his fall from God's grace. He has become an abomination in the eyes of the Lord and he knows too much about our plans. If that boy is at the Willow Springs, I want you to hunt him down and kill him like the dog he is."

T-bone allowed a small smile at his victory. "Yes, Father. I'll take care of everything. You can count on me."

Chapter Six

The tile floors were cool beneath his bare feet as Park moved about his temporary quarters, putting his clothes in the dresser and his laptop on the nightstand. There was no doubt he'd be more comfortable here than on the hard ground several miles away at the campsite they'd half abandoned. Maybe tomorrow he could go back and take down the tent and haul his belongings back to the van. It all would depend on what Cass had Tanner doing to work off his debt.

What was it with all these cowboys and their testosterone-laden strutting?

Not that he had anything against cowboys, because damn those were some good-looking men in the other room. But with all the muscles, guns, and attitude there was no telling how long it would take before he could get Tanner somewhere that people might not try to kill him.

The saboteur. What a strange concept that was. That anyone would deliberately damage the property of another person because they disagreed on lifestyle, on politics, on race. These were not concepts that were part of Park's upbringing. Not that he was naïve, because he'd learned too many ugly things the hard way.

Working with abused children, investigating homes where mothers neglected to buy food so they had money for drugs. Or fathers, when they bothered to stick around, who used their women or children as punching bags. His soul had felt stained the last few years and it had been a quiet desperation eating at him, until he could no longer stay with the agency responsible for overseeing the safety of children. Guilt ate at him, because he knew the cases he left behind were not solved. They were merely handed over to his supervisor, Janet, or to one of the many overworked caseworkers.

Yes, every child deserved to be safe, to be cared for, but it had not been a job Park could do any longer without spiraling into a bottomless depression. There was a reason burnout was high in Child Protective Services.

So what was this weird obsession he was developing with Tanner? By his own admission, the man was a felon, although it appeared, by the grace of Cass Cartwright, he would escape charges. Just because he wasn't going to jail didn't make him less of a criminal.

Cutting fences Park could get over. It wasn't exactly like he was a big supporter of cattle ranchers—but damn, burning down the building? What if someone had been inside or had gotten hurt fighting the fire? Or what if the fire had gotten out of control—this was northern Arizona. The fire danger was real and deadly. And could he really believe that Tanner hadn't intended to hurt Jesse? Or was that just a convenient lapse of memory to be blamed on his injury?

Grabbing his phone, Park flopped onto the bed and crossed his legs. There was only one thing to be done when his mind was in this much turmoil. He pushed speed dial one.

"Hello?"

"Hey, Sunshine," he said to his mother. "How are you? Still kicking ass in canasta?"

His mother's laughter spilled out. "Park! What a nice surprise. How are you? Did you get settled at a new campsite?"

It was Park's turn to laugh. "Not exactly. You're never going to believe what happened." Park explained about the dogs finding an injured Tanner, and the revelations from the meeting he'd just left.

"Park, honey, what aren't you telling me? It sounds as if… Why don't you just tell me?"

"I'm not trying to hide anything, I just don't know what else to say. There's just something about Tanner…and I just met him and he might be a bad person." As the words tumbled out, Park realized just how unsettled the events of the last twenty-four hours had left him.

"Oh, doodlebugs," his mother's said, using his childhood nickname. "Just because he did something bad doesn't mean he's a bad person. From what you've said, it sounds as if he was doing his best to cope with a terrible situation. His father sounds truly troubled."

Park laughed. "Only you would call a total psycho troubled, Mom."

"You know we can't make a diagnosis without actual observation, Park. Listen, sweetheart, you are a social worker by training and a fine observer of human nature. It's clear the Fates led you to find Tanner, he would have died without your help. This sounds to me as if you've found your destiny. I don't suppose you could bring him by…"

"Sunshine," Park said, using his mother's name, hoping to stem the flow of words. "You live twenty-two hundred miles away. That's not exactly an easy-to-swing-by-the-house afternoon drive. Besides, I don't know anything about him yet, let alone know if he's attracted to me—"

"Of course he is—who wouldn't be? Honey, don't overanalyze things. This sounds like a straight-forward fairy tale happily ever after romance. Not that you're straight…although some people would call you a fairy, but I find that such a distasteful term. Gay is so much happier."

Park choked on his laughter.

"Anyway, dear," his mother continued, "I'm afraid there's no getting around this. You must stay close to him. You are responsible for Tanner's life now. It's not possible to say for how long, at least not without a full reading. Do you have the exact date and time of his birth? I'll need the location, too."

A knock at the door drew his attention. "Come in," he called out. "I need to go, Sunshine, someone is here. I'll call in a couple of days and let you know—"

"How the romance is blossoming. Don't hide from this, Park. You can't outrun Fate."

He ended the call and stood to shake hands with his visitor. "Chad, it's good to see you."

"I can honestly say, you are one person I never expected to see at the Willow Springs Ranch." Chad laughed a little. "Jesse caught me up on what happened this morning. I understand you're going to be a guest for a while?"

"It looks like it."

"How about I give you a tour, then?" Chad asked.

"Sure just give me a minute to finish getting ready." As much as he enjoyed the peaceful solitude of primitive camping, he had to admit, it was nice to have access to a well-lighted mirror when putting on his eyeliner. Park retreated to the bathroom and emerged a few minutes later with his long hair twisted into a bun on the top of his head, lids lined.

"I am ready if you are," he said, slipping his feet into his favorite Crocs.

****

It was easier to breathe now that there were only four of them standing close together in Cass's office looking at the map. Too many people had already witnessed his earlier humiliation. Tanner deserved their contempt but that didn't make it any easier to take. He was just grateful that Park wasn't here now, and hadn't been in their room when he'd emerged from the shower wearing clothes borrowed from Chance, of all people. It was only because they were of a similar build, not because Chance had decided to cut him any slack. Tanner couldn't blame the man.

Wearing the borrowed clothes brought forth a whole new reality for him. At this moment, Tanner wasn't any more secure than one of those men pushing a shopping cart through an inner city. In fact, he didn't even have enough belongings to fill a box, let alone a whole cart. There was some money in his bank account and he had access to a small stipend through the trust fund, but for now, he was completely dependent on the charity of neighbors. Charity he didn't deserve.

"Tell me about the bunkers first, Tanner," Chance said. "They seem like the most potential for trouble. Cass, I seriously think we're going to have to let the feds know about this if we can confirm they have underground storage and a weapons cache. That's a lot bigger than a simple feud between neighboring ranches or hate crimes."

"I agree. In fact I'm not sure we shouldn't just go ahead and call right now." Cass was frowning as he stared at the map spread out over a large table.

"Not until we have more information," Ty said.

Tanner leaned forward. "As far as I know, and I think I have the accurate information, there are only two completed bunkers plus two more they plan to finish in the next year, once more of the general's men start to arrive."

"Where are all these people going to live? And is your father the only one here now?"

"Oh no. There are some ranchers in this northeast quadrant who support the general. His followers have bought nearly every property that's been for sale over the last five years from I-40, south. Nearly all the unincorporated parts of east Mohave and west Yavapai counties. But I'll be honest with you, Cass, over the last few months, their support has been dwindling. I think the attempt to subvert the wild horse gather that ended up killing those two BLM wranglers really upset a lot of people.

"Prior to the murders, the separatist movement had pretty good traction because it was an abstract idea. People thought they could band together, refuse to acknowledge the established government, and be left more or less alone. Many people didn't like the violence or the destruction. Plus the work that you and Holden have done to screen the ranch hands has helped a lot of the locals. So maybe that's why the general and my father have ramped up the attacks on the WSR. It just feels more personal now."

"The first bunker is over here," Tanner said, pointing to a hill just south of the far barn on the Trip-T. "You're not going to be able to get to that one and look at it. There are security cameras and trip wires scattered all over. The other one is across the county, on the old Hutchinson property. You follow along the riparian game trail. It's part of the Trip-T grazing area."

"I know exactly where you're talking about," Chance said, looking from the map to Ty. Remember? It's got that piece of shit shack we searched when we were looking for Bryan."

"Yep. Son of a bitch. We never went back and checked it out."

"No, because we tipped the feds," Chance said. "It was better for us to just stay out of the way. Is there anybody out there?"

Tanner shook his head. "There was too much interest in the area after the murders, even though the bodies were found on the other side of the county. The bunker idea is on the back burner for now—like I said, they decided to focus on that next year."

"Feel like taking a ride?" Chance asked Ty. "If we leave while it's still daylight, it looks like a recreational ride. We can take a casual look around."

Ty turned to Cass. "What do you think?"

"Tanner, how certain are you that no one's out there?" Cass asked, his brows drawn together in a deep frown.

"I just rode through there the other day, but I can't promise you that my brother T-bone won't be in the area. It's Trip-T grazing land, and he's the type to shoot first and defend himself to the law later. Still, it's very low priority for us—them—right now. They don't want to draw any attention to that part of the ranch."

"Tell me about T-bone," Ty said.

"I think—he's crazy. He's pushing my father to the brink with his comments about the WSR, gays, federal interference. You name it. I think he's hoping to be the general's second in command. Or maybe even take over someday. He's threatened to expose—" The words got lodged in his throat and he looked toward the only door as if escape were an option. He didn't miss the look the other three men shared.

Cass straightened from where he'd been hunched over the map and met his gaze. "Tanner, you're safe here. If what you're about to say is that T-bone threatened to expose you for being gay…well, there isn't anybody here who will judge you."

"I'm not—I mean I haven't." Tanner cleared his throat, the heat in his cheeks like a bad sunburn. "Tim doesn't know shit, but he was always threatening to tell our father. All this stuff about the general just plays into my father's homophobia. Sometimes I think that's the whole reason he hooked up with the separatist movement. He's said more than once that being homosexual makes someone an abomination. He has it all tied up in religion and prejudice and hate. I guarantee you that if my father thought I was gay, he'd have me killed."

"That's not going to happen," Ty said quietly. He looked at Cass and some silent communication passed between the two men then Cass nodded once.

"Tanner, every man here has a story to tell. Some of us were free to be ourselves, but many of the men here faced obstacles growing up or even as adults. It looks to me like you're gonna be spending a lot of time around us on the WSR. I know there're a lot of rumors about what happens out here, but not every man who works here is gay. Some are. Others are bisexual and others just don't give a shit. Who you love or who you fuck is your business. The only rule is we respect each other. Can you live with that?" Cass asked.

"Yes, sir."

Ty laughed. "Take that old man."

"Effective immediately we have a new rule. No calling me sir," Cass said. "Ty, I think it's a good idea for you and Chance to take a ride, but no unnecessary risks. You got that?"

"Yes, sir," Ty grinned.

"Fuck you," Cass said on a laugh.

"Later, if you're lucky," Ty shot back. "Chance and I will be back in a couple of hours. I need someone to keep an eye on dinner, I've got trays of lasagna ready to go in the oven."

"I can do that."

Tanner's attention swung to the doorway, where Park stood with a short blond man. A Park who looked very different from the man he'd met yesterday and spent the morning with. Tanner scanned from the bun, to the makeup, to the—he blinked—pink plastic shoes. "Ho-ly shit."

Chapter Seven

Tanner was tired deep in his bones. The stress over the last several days combined with the residual effects of his injuries took a toll. He was fairly certain the day had been the longest in his life. After the meeting with Cass, Tanner had been examined by Bryan, Chance's partner, who had pronounced he would live. Then the former Navy Corpsman promptly ordered him to take some pain relievers and rest. Which of course hadn't happened because there were apologies to make and damages to assess.

The first apology after the meeting had been to Chad Ollom, the man leading Park on a tour of the WSR. As the ranch construction foreman, he was the most directly effected by the fire Tanner had set to the unfinished dorm. Chad had already started ordering the replacement materials to rebuild the bunkhouse. Along with a sincere apology, Tanner had asked permission from Cass to work with Chad on the construction. Cass hadn't even hesitated—in fact the man had seemed pleased that Tanner asked. He'd offered another apology to both Chad and Jesse for the pain he'd caused, then walked around the main compound to meet with as many of the other ranch hands as he could find. Once he'd made the rounds, he'd asked to meet privately with Cass once more.

"I know I don't deserve—" he'd started to say, but Cass cut him off.

"Tanner, there are damn few people in life who don't deserve a second chance, but just because we're opening the door, doesn't mean all is forgiven. You have to earn trust and that's going to take time."

Despite the warning in those words, he'd offered to let Tanner have use of one of the ranch trucks so he could go to Kingman in the next few days and get his own clothes and other personal supplies. Cass was being far more generous to him than he deserved and Tanner vowed he would not let the older man down. He didn't know what would become of his father or his brother once Chance called federal law enforcement, but he understood there was no real choice. The things that the general and his own family had done were far beyond any tolerable activity.

Moving slowly, Tanner made his way to his assigned guest room and tried not to think about his temporary roommate. Cass's overwhelming generosity had made it impossible for Tanner to request his own room. He just hadn't felt comfortable asking for any more favors today. Now, with the long night stretching in front of him, all Tanner wanted to do was take a hot shower, more ibuprofen, and close his eyes for the next twelve hours. Tomorrow would be soon enough to deal with the misunderstanding and Park.

Since Park was in the kitchen helping Ty with the cleanup, this was the best time to take advantage of the hot shower in their en suite guest room. The shower he'd taken earlier had done its job, if you only counted removing the blood and dirt from his three days in the wilderness. But it had been hurried by the knowledge Cass and the others were waiting to hear his information about the bunkers. Now he planned to let water as hot as he could stand it loosen the tightness in his sore muscles. Stripping quickly from the borrowed shirt and jeans, Tanner examined himself in the bathroom mirror.

The wound on the side of his head was the worst of his injuries. Black, purple, blue, and fading yellow around the edges did not make a very attractive picture. His right eye was slightly swollen, and the bruise extended below his lower lid. There were scratches on his hands, face, and neck, as if he'd dragged himself along the hard-packed dirt. He supposed he had, otherwise there was no way to explain how he'd covered so much ground between the site of the attack and where Park had found him. He wished he could remember more about what happened.

Standing nude before the mirror, there was no place to hide, and yet, he wasn't sure he knew who he was anymore. Familiar brown eyes looked back at him. Not even twenty-four, yet the lines around his eyes and the tired expression made him look like a much older man. Which was really strange, considering being here on the WSR made him feel much younger than his years. These men were far more experienced in life beyond their ranch. They'd traveled, held important jobs, and embraced their sexuality. How pathetic was it that the most sexually exciting experience of his life had been holding Park's cock first thing this morning?

Tanner's own dick felt heavy and started to stiffen at the memory.

"That would be your cue to stop standing here staring at yourself and get in the damn shower, Triplett," he said. Then he turned quickly toward the door, making sure he was really alone. Did other people speak out loud when they were by themselves? God, what was wrong with him? Park would think he was crazy if he came into the bedroom and heard him talking. Was he really this socially backward?

For the last five years, his life had revolved completely around the Trip-T, ranching, and his father's causes. Since Trip's beliefs ran counter to Tanner's true nature, that had meant hiding every part of himself from those who surrounded him.

Once, he'd had a dream. He would work on his land, raising Quarter Horses, training cutters for other ranchers. But when he'd finished school and spent more time around the Trip-T and his father, the beginnings of the dementia became clear. Hell, call it what it was—his old man was bat shit crazy. For far too long, he'd allowed himself to be sucked into the madness in some horribly misguided attempt at damage control.

The fact was the only real damage he'd been trying to minimize was to his dream. He'd wanted his father to keep it together long enough for Tanner to claim his full inheritance and save the ranch for future generations of Tripletts. That dream was well and truly gone now. He wasn't sure about all the legalities, but his family's land would no doubt be confiscated in whatever action the government took against them.

No more hiding anything, now. The case would be against all of them. Tanner had been involved in the sabotage, had allowed the planning to continue without protesting—had been a full participant—that made him just as responsible as his brother, his father, the general.

With a deep sigh, Tanner went to the freestanding tub and turned on the faucet. Modified with exposed pipes, a large showerhead, and a curtain mounted from the ceiling, the old fashioned tub would accommodate the modern preference most people had for showers. After a brief hesitation, he reached for the rubber stopper and turned the water hotter. A soak would feel even better. His legs were so tired, they practically shook with fatigue.

With a hand on the wall for balance, Tanner carefully stepped into the deep, over-sized bath with a grin. Although it might have appeared out of place at first, someone understood long-legged cowboys with saddle-weary muscles. Continuing to hold on for support, Tanner slowly lowered into the water. Once the tub was full, he turned off the faucet and leaned back with a groan that was half-pain and half-relief.

As he soaked, each small movement caused the water to lap at his skin, easing his aches. Reaching for the washcloth and a bar of soap, he worked up a good lather. Still moving slowly, he ran the cloth over his chest, the wet terrycloth rough as he swiped it over his nipples. He groaned again, remembering the feel of his chest against Park's smooth back. Then he pictured the exotic look of the other man this afternoon, tightly restrained hair, beautiful eyes wide, his gaze returning to Tanner over and over. His fingers twitched with desire to take Park's hair down and let it spill over the both of them.

Dropping the idea of washing in favor of a much more pressing need, Tanner pinched and twisted each of his nips until they ached. God…what would it feel like to have another man touch him? Taste him?

He traced his fingers lower, damp hair soft, his skin sensitive. Trailing over his ribs, along his lower belly, light touches that brushed against the tops of his thighs, then back to his hips. Gripping his cock, he wasn't even going to lie to himself. The idea of being with another man just flat out did it for him. Waking with Park's cock in his hand this morning was more than a nice memory, it was rapidly becoming an obsession.

Sliding his hand along his shaft, Tanner added some lather, then began to move faster. Closing his eyes, the cock in his hand became Park's. He worked his lover, the grip firm, the pace quick. He swiped his thumb over the leaking crown, then added an extra twist on each upstroke. His balls drew up, tight, hard, close. Hips rocking in time with his hand, Tanner whispered his fantasy lover's name as he gripped tighter, imagining his cock in Park's ass.

Tanner's head dropped back against the porcelain and a surprised grunt escaped at his sudden climax. Cum shot onto his chest, his body in total lockdown, as his muscles contracted and released in waves of pleasure.

****

Park hadn't meant to intrude, but after Ty summarily dismissed him from the kitchen, there hadn't been much else to do except return to his bedroom. Besides, there were things he wanted to discuss with Tanner, elements about his father's condition and questions about any plans he might have been involved in—because there could be some serious repercussions. Not that he thought Tanner was stupid by any stretch of the imagination, but he'd spent the day wondering about his naiveté.

The events of the day revealed a man who had been raised in an environment that in no way would've been healthy for raising a gay teen. And even if he hadn't awakened this morning with his cock in Tanner's hand, the time they'd spent here on the WSR left little doubt that Tanner was interested in other men. Not that he'd done anything inappropriate, it was more the way his gaze lingered whenever he was in the vicinity of any of the gay couples they'd encountered. Especially the wistful expression on his face as he'd watched Cass and Ty when the latter returned safely from the scouting mission.

The initial impulse to protect Tanner was even stronger than it had been earlier, yet he no longer felt his new friend was in any danger from the men of the WSR. In fact, once the initial confrontation was over, Cass seemed to be willing to take Tanner in and offer his protection. Which probably meant Park insisting they share a room for Tanner's safety was inappropriate. Since Tanner hadn't asked to change the arrangement, Park wasn't about to either.

Now, Park stood, his hand on the bathroom doorknob, his pulse racing. Everything about this screamed bad idea, yet he was completely unable to turn away from the erotic sound of Tanner as he clearly pleasured himself in the tub. Low moans, the gentle splash of water, the distinctive sound of a wet hand sliding on bare flesh. Pressing his forehead to the door, Park closed his eyes, picturing the bigger man, the broad, furred chest, long legs, narrow hips, and tight ass. What was it with all these cowboys?

The sounds from the other side of the door grew louder, then he heard a sharp intake of breath and his own name whispered in that deep sexy voice. Unable or unwilling to resist, Park turned the knob and looked inside.

A very wet Tanner lay in the old-fashioned tub, his body flushed, hand gripping his cock as cum pulsed across his chest. The mental image of a few moments earlier paled in comparison to the perfection of the big man. Park stepped inside and closed the door quietly, hoping that the brush of air wouldn't interrupt Tanner before he was finished.

With another sexy moan, Tanner's body relaxed, his grip loosening, lids slowly opening. His head rolled to the right, and it took less than a second before his eyes flew open and every muscle started to tense all over again.

"Oh fuck…" Tanner said. His voice was a harsh whisper.

"Oh God, I hope so. But you're driving."

Tanner's eyes widened, but his fingers and cock both twitched. Park forced himself away long enough to retrieve one of the oversized bath towels. Turning back to the tub, he held out his hand. "Come on, Tanner. Let's take the discussion to the bedroom. I'd hate to have certain of your body parts shrivel while we sort things out."

Tanner blinked up at him, then releasing his cock, he splashed water over his chest, washing away the evidence of his solo activity. His gaze dropped to

Park's bulging crotch, then slowly back up until they were staring at each other.

"I don't—" Tanner cleared his throat. "I've never been with anyone."

"Your pace here, Tanner. Let me show you…"

Nodding once, Tanner pushed himself to his feet, then leaned down to pull the plug.

Park moaned at the sight of those wet, tight ass cheeks. He wanted to run his tongue over every part of that beautiful body, teach Tanner the pleasures to be shared between men. He helped Tanner stay balanced as he stepped from the tub, then quickly dried him, without lingering, despite his overwhelming need and Tanner's obviously growing desire. When he finished the cursory pass, he wrapped the towel around Tanner's back and used it to pull him closer.

For a long minute, he wondered if Tanner would bolt, then the bigger man lowered his mouth to take a quick kiss. He pulled slightly back, scanning Park's face. "Is this more of that kismet you were talking about?"

Park smiled. "No doubt."

"Where are the dogs?" Tanner asked.

Park laughed. He could easily fall for a man who could kiss while naked and still remember there were dogs to consider.

"Jesse and Chad took them to their casita. Said something about not wanting to disturb your rest."

Tanner flushed, but lowered his head once again. The next kiss was harder, because their teeth bumped as they each shifted their heads to find the right angle, and Park fought against another laugh that threatened to ruin the moment. Then just like the Fates, everything aligned and their tongues slid together. Tanner's mouth was hot, his taste a little spicy, the kiss delicious. The scent of the man, the soap, the shampoo lingered around them and made Park aware that he needed to clean up too.

Breaking the kiss, Park leaned back. "Mmm…so nice. Will you wait for me in the bedroom? I just need a minute to clean up."

Tanner stepped back and took the towel from Park's hands. "Change your mind?"

"Hardly. But I've been traveling for a couple of days and I'd really like a quick shower. Three minutes, I promise."

"Okay, but leave the eyeliner."

Park grinned as Tanner turned and headed for the bedroom.

*

It might've been closer to five minutes than three, but when he stepped out of the bathroom, hair and body clean, with a fresh application of eyeliner, Tanner was laid across the double bed like a holiday feast. As much as Park preferred to keep his own body manscaped, he couldn't deny the beauty of the natural

89

look of his soon-to-be lover. He'd never been much for bar scenes, his lovers were coworkers or businessmen, an occasional buddy fuck with a friend. Safe, sane, and definitely experienced—Park wasn't into risky hook ups, despite the impression some got from his flighty appearance. He liked a man who knew what he was doing, who could respect him outside the bedroom, but took charge and drove hard once the clothes were off.

This cowboy intrigued him for all the wrong reasons. A closeted virgin? Ah, well. Any chance of walking away existed only in the realm of make-believe, because there was no way he could resist sampling from the buffet before him.

Tanner's muscular body was spectacular. Well, except for a few nasty bruises, but there were a lot of things Park wanted to hold against the other man other than some temporary imperfections. Naked and sprawled across the bed, Tanner's broad shoulders led to a well-formed chest, his pecs covered with soft-looking brown hair that vee'd along his belly. The trail of hair led lower—straight to an untrimmed thatch nesting around Tanner's thick cock.

"Don't move a muscle," Park said. He went to his bag and brought out a small bottle of lube and a couple of foil packets. Not a Boy Scout, just prepared. He climbed straight onto the bed, positioning himself at Tanner's side. *All the better to eat you, my dear.* Pushing lines from Little Red Riding Hood firmly from his mind, Park leaned down for his first taste of the lightly-tanned skin.

Just like the kiss, there was a spicy, almost earthy flavor that could easily become addictive. He licked at the flat copper nipple closest to him, tugging the pebbled nub into his mouth. Tanner's sharp intake of breath turned into a soft moan. Park rubbed his cheek against the silky hair of Tanner's chest, moving to give the other nipple the same attention. Tanner's engorged cock bobbed, now fully recovered from his bath time activities and demanding attention. Park licked his lips.

Following the fine trail of hair below Tanner's navel, he met the thick cock with his tongue, swiping at the bead of pre-cum, before swallowing the broad cap. He slowly licked the thick vein on the underside of Tanner's cock with the flat of his tongue, reveling in the way the broad shoulders came off the bed.

"Oh Jesus," Tanner whispered. Rough hands twisted into his hair as he sucked Tanner fully into his mouth. Without letting up on the suction, he shifted on his knees to move between Tanner's legs. Opening his jaws wide, Park took Tanner's cock faster and deep enough to bump against the back of his throat with each hard stroke.

"Oh holy—" Tanner gasped. "Please…Park. Can I fuck you?" he asked, tugging on Park's shoulders to force him to pull back from the blow job.

Park sat back on his haunches with a satisfied hum. There were just no finer words to his mind than those. Finesse? Never heard the word. Patience? Deserted him. He asked what he needed to know. "This is really your first time?"

Tanner flushed a deep red beneath his tan. "I've watched porn, I know how the parts fit."

Park reached for the lube and tossed the condom onto Tanner's flat stomach. "Good. Glove up."

Tanner tore open the foil packet, his hands shaking slightly, but he managed to roll the condom over his no doubt sensitive shaft before he looked back at Park.

Tanner's lids were heavy, sexy, but they widened when Park poured a generous amount of slick on his fingers, then reached back to prep his own ass. Usually, Park enjoyed a lover who took his time, who cared enough to make sure they both enjoyed the experience—but he had a feeling neither of them was going to last long this first round. And even if it was already the second for Tanner, he wanted to make sure he had that thick cock inside his ass before the other man shot again.

Tanner watched for a minute, chewed his lower lip, then reach for the bottle of lube and poured some into his right hand. Slowly, he stroked himself, never looking away from where Park's fingers worked his own ass.

"Doing okay? A little nervous?" Park asked

"Uh…yes. Maybe. Yes."

"Sorry, I should have let you explore. Next time. I mean we're probably going to be here for a few days, right? That is, if you don't mind sharing the room. There's a lot more than a just quick—" Park broke off as Tanner's eyes drifted closed. He wasn't asleep, he was sure of that, but his chiseled features relaxed except for a small crease between his brows. "Damn, you don't say much, do you, Tanner? Still with me?"

"Trying to hold on. That's too fucking sexy to watch. Besides, you were kind of doing enough talking for both of us. Not much dialog in porn."

Park laughed. "Point taken. Ready?"

Nodding, Tanner gripped his cock, pointing it straight up, while Park straddled his hips. "I'm going to control the pace, but don't worry. It's not going to hurt except in a good way." Watching Tanner's expressive face, he pressed his slick opening against the broad tip, a steady pressure that yielded when his ass opened and Tanner breached him. Tanner's gaze shifted to where they were joined then back up to search Park's face.

"You're okay?" he asked, his voice a husky whisper.

Park sucked in a quick breath, lifted, lowered, lifted once more, before sinking fully, his ass stretched to the limit. "Yeah, give me a sec," he moaned.

After a minute, he started to rock, loosening his muscles even further. Then Park was moving, his quads pumping up, his control nearly shot by the overwhelming fullness and a need for more. Harder. Faster.

As if catching his sense of urgency, Tanner slid his hands along Park's thighs to grab his ass, his biceps bulging as he took over the responsibility for rocking them together in a steady rhythm. Tanner raised and lowered Park, thrust his hips, then pulled back, his cock gliding in, then nearly out of Park's ass. They moved like that for long minutes, skin slapping against skin until they were both coated in a fine sheen of sweat as they worked hard to keep up the pounding pace. Park began to rock faster, his breath labored. He gripped his cock, his hand still slick, sliding hard and fast, matching their pace.

"So good, Tanner," he gasped. "Close."

Tanner grunted, but after a few more hard thrusts, his hips stuttered and his cock stalled deep inside. Park greedily watched Tanner's face as he came. His head arched back, eyes closed, lower lip caught between his teeth. Then Park's ass clenched as his own orgasm pulsed hot between them, stripes of creamy white painting Tanner's chest.

Even as his ass continued to spasm, Tanner loosened his grip on Park's hips, rough hands scraping along Park's forearms, before reaching his shoulders. Then he pulled Park down into a searing kiss. Their mouths crashed together in a tangle of lips, teeth, and tongue. They stayed that way, kissing, tasting, fused together until the need to breathe was too great, and they broke apart, both gasping for air.

Park kissed Tanner lightly once more before raising himself up. "Wait here…"

"Movement's an option?" Tanner mumbled. His lips were swollen from their kisses, dark brown eyes mostly hidden beneath heavy lids, face slack with pleasure.

Park returned to the bed a few minutes later, bringing a warm cloth. With a smile, he cleaned his cum from the sleeping Tanner's stomach, then pulled the bedspread up. Sliding under the covers, he tucked himself close to Tanner's side. As if they belonged, Tanner rolled over and wrapped an arm over Park's side, very much like they'd started the day.

His own lids grew heavy, exhaustion claiming him, and he melted back into the embrace. A funny thing happened on his way to the land of Nod. A ball of regret formed in his belly. Not over where he was or who he was with—no way. Tanner was exactly who he'd been looking for. And that was what caused him to pause.

How could two so very different people have anything except a passing attraction for each other? And if this was more…shouldn't he have made sure Tanner's first time was more…special? Then the worries slid away as he tumbled over the edge and into sleep.

Chapter Eight

"Good morning, Ty. Mind if I come in?" Tanner asked, stepping into the kitchen in the early morning stillness of the house.

The blue-eyed gaze snapped up and considered him for a long moment, before Tyler gave a quick nod. "You're up early. I don't usually see the first ranch hands in here for coffee for another forty-five minutes. Do you have something planned—or were you just trying to escape before Park wakes up?"

Ty continued to stare and damn if he didn't feel his cheeks heat under the other man's scrutiny. Ignoring Ty's implication, Tanner made his way to the industrial-sized coffee maker. The stainless steel urn gurgled, but the orange indicator light refused to acknowledge his desperate need for coffee. Tanner sighed.

"It'll be ready in about five minutes," Ty said. "Grab a mug and help yourself to the pot on the stove. If I had to wait for that beast to finish before I got my first cup of coffee, then breakfast wouldn't be ready until noon."

"Oh, thank God," Tanner said. Removing a mug from the tray on the counter, Tanner poured himself a large serving of hot, dark coffee. It had been four days since his last morning cup of joe, and that was entirely too long. Holding the cup in both hands, he breathed in the rich aroma. Unable to wait another minute, he blew over the surface then took a quick sip. "Ouch, shit. Hot."

Ty laughed. "Need the caffeine that bad?"

Tanner nodded, and sipped again, then moved to stand near the counter, unsure how welcome he would be in the kitchen during breakfast preparation.

Ty stepped to the stove and topped off his own mug, then set it aside, untasted. After a glance at the clock, he walked over to a tall rack in the corner of the kitchen and removed two trays of buttermilk biscuits, placing them side-by side on the counter. "Make yourself useful. Take this pastry brush and put a little melted butter on the top of each biscuit. When you're done, put them in the oven and set the timer. I like to have a little something for the men to grab with their coffee when they head out for the first round of chores. Meals are at nine, noon, and six."

"Okay." Tanner did as directed, keeping an eye on Ty as the big man worked at the stove. In addition to the old-fashioned coffee pot, there was a batch of gravy simmering in a deep pot and the griddle sizzled with a couple of dozen sausage patties. It seemed like a lot more than a grab and go. At the Trip-T, the men were on their own for meals. Of course there were only half a dozen working there these days. His father's outside interests had cost the ranch a serious amount of money in recent years and they would soon be out of the Quarter Horse business altogether.

As Ty moved easily between the tasks, it seemed as if he tracked everything at once. "Local gossip has you as a Navy SEAL. Where'd you learn to cook?" Tanner asked, curious about this man who by all accounts hadn't been raised around ranching.

"In the Navy. Back in the day, men selected for SEAL duty came from a variety of other ratings. Listen, let's not waste this quiet time talking about my past. I know you didn't voice any objection to sharing a room with Park last night, but everything was sort of confusing yesterday. Are you okay? Do you need to…you know…talk about anything?"

Heat crawled up his face again and Tanner carefully studied the biscuits he was painting. He hoped like hell Ty wasn't looking at him, because his blush would be a dead giveaway. A big hand landed on his wrist, stilling his movement and forcing him to meet the man's gaze.

"Tanner, no matter how bad things were at home, you're on the WSR now. You're not alone."

"It's just hard to explain…" How did you make someone understand what it felt like to listen to your father spew hate about people who were just like you?

To never be able to show your true self around the very people you should always be able to count on?

Ty nodded at him, but released his arm and stepped back. He cleared his throat. "When I was a kid, my dad made my life a living hell because I was gay. The details aren't important, but on my seventeenth birthday, he took me to a recruiter and signed his permission for me to join. He said the Navy would make a man out of me. The policy might be gone now, but Don't Ask Don't Tell ruled my life until I met Cass. I understand not showing who you are to the rest of the world."

"Shit." Tanner's gaze met Ty's briefly before he looked away and reached for his mug.

"Yeah. Shit," Ty continued. "People can do fucked up things to each other, but I'm living proof that it's never too late to…come to terms with who you are." Ty shrugged. "I'm gay. Big fucking deal. It wasn't like I didn't know—there was just a lot of shit in the way. It kept me from being myself for too long."

"Uhm…how old were you when you first had s—" Embarrassed by the question he'd half asked, but fascinated by the similarities in their stories, Tanner watched as Ty looked over to the doorway for a moment.

"Cass was my first lover," he said at last.

Damn, he'd only met Cass last year. There must be a helluva lot more to the story—but he was grateful to the man for sharing something so personal. It left him feeling the need to return the confidence. Not anything about Park, because he wasn't ready to deal with that in his own mind, let alone discuss it with a relative stranger. Still, Ty had been honest with him about coming out. He swallowed hard, then took the plunge. "I'm…uh…gay, too," he said. His voice was a strangled whisper.

"Yeah, I sort of gathered that from some of the talk yesterday. That must have been hell with your father and brother being total 'phobes. I don't know much about…T-bone?"

Relieved at the shift and opportunity to talk about something else, Tanner nodded. "Yeah. His real name is Timothy."

"How old are you? And is he younger or older?"

"I'm twenty-three—the oldest of three boys. Tim is four years younger, but he's closest to our father." The conversation seemed to die out as Tanner turned back to finish the biscuits and Ty returned to the stove.

They worked in a companionable silence for a few minutes, then Ty cleared his throat again with a fake sounding cough. "So about Park…do you have any, uh, questions?"

Tanner blinked, turned to face the other man, then laughter spilled out. "Oh my god. Is this a sex talk? Did you get the short straw?"

Ty flushed. "Fuck. Sorry. It's just we put you in a room with a man you just met, and it occurred to me that could be goddamn awkward under the best of circumstances. So if you want another room tonight, just say so."

"No, uh…we're good," he said, quickly turning back to the biscuits. "I'm ready to put these in the oven. How long should I set the timer for?"

"Good morning."

Tanner looked up to find Park standing in the arched entryway that separated the kitchen and dining room. His heart skipped several beats as his eyes feasted. Waves of blond cascaded around his shoulders, spilling over the worn-looking Grateful Dead tee shirt. He wore a fresh pair of faded jeans, his long bare feet peeking out from the frayed hems. Park was such a crazy throwback to the sixties—a counterculture decade that would have passed unacknowledged on the Trip-T. He would have told anyone who asked, that a free-spirited man like Park was just not his type. Not that Tanner had a type, because…well, you had to date a few guys and look around before you knew what you wanted. Didn't you? Then his gaze began the slow trip back up Park's body, before he got stuck on the obvious bulge behind Park's fly.

"Jesus Christ," Ty said, directly behind him, making Tanner jump. "You two need to take that look somewhere else before you set my kitchen on fire."

"Morning, Ty," Cass said, coming through the back door with a bang, drawing everyone's attention the other direction.

"Great. Grand fucking Central," Ty muttered, but he was smiling as he went straight to Cass for a kiss. "Everything okay? You went out early…" he said.

Remembering he hadn't even returned Park's greeting, Tanner turned back, without bothering to listen to Cass's answer. Park was staring at him, his expression neutral, maybe even a little guarded.

"Hey, good morning," Tanner said, with a smile.

"Is it?" Park asked. "I thought—" The back door banged again, and they turned to see Chance step inside.

Making straight for the coffee urn, he said, "Oh, good, you're all here. We need to talk."

****

Damn…all he'd wanted this morning was a few minutes alone to talk with Tanner, to make sure everything was okay. Not every man reacted well to his first time. Although, there hadn't been anything tentative about the loving last night. Park fought against yet another flood of desire as he tried to focus on whatever it was Chance had to say.

"I've thought about this all last night, even called a buddy of mine and ran a few scenarios past him. There's not much wiggle room here, guys. These are serious federal charges we're talking about," Chance said. He took up the conversation from yesterday afternoon, as if there hadn't been a break.

"If all the...what the fuck are they called? The Armed Resistance Militia...if all they'd been discussing was a petition to secede, then it wouldn't be any big deal. I mean hell, a hundred thousand people signed a petition for Texas to secede and the short answer is no. But it isn't illegal to ask, right?"

Cass nodded but all Park could manage was a blink.

Chance sipped his coffee while the rest of them moved to huddle around the kitchen counter. Park took a position right next to Tanner, but refrained from wrapping an arm around his waist. Despite the lingering look Ty teased them about, he was pretty sure Tanner wasn't ready for any public displays of affection.

"From what Tanner here was telling us, these men want to create a separate sovereign nation, and are willing to engage in armed conflict to make that happen. This is conceivably domestic terrorism—an anarchist militia plotting to overthrow the government. And because he was involved in the discussions and the action, our boy Tanner is culpable."

"I thought you said the bunker was empty yesterday?" asked Cass. "Do you think they'll find some more evidence?"

"It was empty, but the feds will bring in forensic experts. They'll be looking for fingerprints and trace evidence of explosives, blood, et cetera. Anything that shows if—or how—the bunker was used. Look, these are massive investigations, and there is virtually nothing they will leave untouched."

Tanner's face was pale, his mouth a grim line, but he stood with his back straight, head held high. "I realized when I came here there would be consequences. I'm prepared."

"You know, Tanner," Park said quietly, putting his hand on Tanner's shoulder. "I really think it would be in your best interest to keep quiet right now. How about we get the dogs and head to Flagstaff. I know a lawyer—"

"Hold that thought, Park," Chance said. "I've got—"

Park stiffened. "I am not about to let you railroad—"

"Everybody hang on a sec." Cass held up his hand, forestalling any further discussion. "At any minute, a dozen cowboys are going to wander through looking for coffee before they hit their chores, and there is one pissed off cook glaring daggers at me." He turned to face Park directly. "Chance isn't trying to railroad Tanner, he's looking for a way to save his ass."

Cass shifted his gaze to Tanner. "Park's right, though, you do need an attorney before we do anything official, right, Chance?"

"Absolutely. That's what I was about to say. Because my sources say the feds have been sniffing all over this area ever since the BLM wranglers were killed, but everything pointed to Hutchinson as the killer. They might believe there were more people involved, but they didn't have any evidence. Ty, you finish what you're doing here, we'll head into the office. Join us when you can?"

*

As if they hadn't taken the brief break to change locations, Chance started speaking almost as soon as they were in the office. The four of them gathered around the table still covered by the maps of the WSR, and Park stared at the blue circles marking the spots where Tanner confessed to cutting the fence line to release some of the cattle. Feeling queasy, he shifted his gaze and found Tanner staring at him, lips pressed together, the corners of his mouth turned down. He wanted to tell him it was okay, to reassure his lover that he wasn't judging. Not exactly. Then Chance cleared his throat and the moment slipped away.

"Tanner, I'm being as flat out honest as I know how. We both know there is enough evidence now to put your ass away—and the fact that I'm in this room means Cass has decided he doesn't want that to happen. There's a reason Cass has me working on this instead of Holden. Our former sheriff is a good man, but my black and white aren't nearly as clear-cut as his."

Tanner lifted his head and looked at the tall rancher. They stared at each other a long moment before Cass nodded once, then Cass briefly met Park's gaze before turning to face Chance once again.

"The way I figure it, you have two choices if you don't want to spend the rest of your life in jail. You can run...I mean like right-the-fuck-now. Get in Park's van and get the hell out of here. You'll need new ID and you can't ever contact your family or friends around here. As soon as you—"

"I'm not running," Tanner interrupted, voice flat and eyes narrowed.

"Good man," Cass murmured.

Chance nodded, flashed a quick smile, then continued, "Then you're going to have to turn your family in. Provide the evidence that the government needs to get warrants, probably testify in court. In my opinion, you need an attorney first, though. Before you talk to anyone."

Cass nodded. "As soon as it's a decent hour, I'll call Cade and Carter in Flagstaff. The sooner we can—"

Tanner's freshly-charged cell phone buzzed, the sound carrying clearly. He yanked the clip from his belt and checked the caller ID. "Flagstaff Regional Medical Center?" he said. "Who could be calling... Hello?"

Park ran his hand down Tanner's back while the big man listened. He shot out questions, listened some more, nodding as if the person on the other end of the connection could see him. "I'll be there as quickly as I can, but I'm about four hours away. Tell him…to hang on."

"What's happened?" Park asked.

"My dad and brother were in a car accident, just past Seligman on I-40. I…uh…a semi jackknifed right in front of them. They said Tim was driving…he didn't make it. Dad was Lifelined to Flagstaff. He's in surgery now. My brother Thomas lives in Flag and is on his way, but, uh—I've got to…" Tanner looked around.

"Are you sure the call is legit? Call back, see if it's really the hospital," Chance said.

Tanner nodded and hit redial. They all heard the operator's voice. "Flagstaff Regional Medical Center, how may I direct your call?" Tanner glanced around the room. "I'm calling about an accident victim." He relayed the information from the previous call, but hung up shortly after. "They can't give me information by phone until he's transferred to a room or a family member is present to update the status of a surgery in progress. Look, the call came from the hospital, it's damned hard to fake caller id on a legitimate number. I need to go."

"I'll take you, honey," Park said. "You shouldn't be alone, shouldn't drive."

"Take one of the ranch trucks," Cass offered. "We'll take care of your dogs."

Park looked at Tanner as he clipped the phone back to his waistband. The man seemed to be moving in slow motion. Cass stepped forward and tugged on his arm.

"Tanner, you don't worry about anything we've talked about this morning until after you find out about your father. I'm going to follow through with my lawyers. You can meet with them once your dad is stable…before you leave Flagstaff. Tanner, don't say a word about this to anyone."

"I'll make sure," Park said. He considered it a vow.

*

Less than thirty minutes later, having declined the offer of one of the ranch's gas-hogging monster trucks, Park drove his van over the bumps and ruts in the dirt road leading from the WSR back to the main highway that would eventually end at the interstate. Tanner stared out the side window, absently fingering his cell phone, probably waiting for more bad news.

"Tanner? You okay?" Park asked just before they made the turn off from the WSR property.

There was a heavy sigh, then Tanner turned to face him. "Yeah. I'm okay. But this is all so fucked up."

Park glanced quickly over, then back at the road. He thought he knew a little about what was happening in Tanner's head. "Tanner, stop. Don't take on any guilt that doesn't belong to you."

"What's that supposed to mean?" There was an edge to Tanner's question, but Park blew through any warning signs.

"It's pretty simple. You're sitting over there wondering which event in the last twenty-four hours you could change that would alter what happened to your brother and father, right?"

"What if I am? I should have sent you on your way and confronted T-bone yesterday morning. Or at least gone to the Trip-T and told my father…at least made an effort to reason with him."

"Nothing about your decision to come to the Willow Springs caused this accident. Nothing you told Cass or Chance. You are not responsible. And while we're at it, there's nothing we did last night that caused this accident either."

"Is that what you believe? Really? Then explain your whole kismet, karma, Age of Aquarius bullshit. Because right now, I'm seeing a fucking black hole in your logic that's big enough to drive the Enterprise through."

Park's eyes went wide with shock and he nearly stomped on the brake as he turned to meet Tanner's angry gaze. "Are you kidding me? In the middle of this nightmare you pull out Star Trek humor? Are you trying to make me love you?"

As if his words needed some sort of cosmic exclamation point, there was a giant clap of thunder and his van went airborne amidst a storm of dirt and rocks. He reached for Tanner with his right hand, as if he could possibly prevent him from flying through the windshield as the van twisted and tilted on an invisible fulcrum to perform some weird double axle.

109

In a blinding moment of absolute clarity, Park knew three things. He loved Tanner. T-bone was alive. They were going to die. Then his head connected with the steering wheel, and he knew no more.

Chapter Nine

Tyler scraped the lightly sautéed onions from his skillet into a stainless steel baking pan. Turning back to the stove, he added mushrooms to the still-hot frying pan. As they began to cook, he took up his knife and chopped the multi-colored bell peppers. The egg casserole was a meal that required no thought because he'd made it so often in the past. Once he added the vegetables, he would pour in five-dozen lightly beaten eggs. After the casserole cooked long enough to set the eggs, he would add biscuits and cheese as a topping. The men loved it, and it would give him enough time to join the others in the office. Something about Tanner's situation really tugged at Tyler. It brought up memories of his own unhappy childhood, and while neither of their fathers may have been physically abusive, there was no denying the emotional abuse they'd both learned to deal with.

His father might have forced him to join, but Ty had embraced the Navy once he enlisted. It had been the very best thing that had ever happened to him. Well, before coming to the WSR and meeting Cass. Given Tanner's heritage and the knowledge that one day the Trip-T would be his—despite his father's current control—it was easy to understand how one small step to preserve his future inheritance led to another small step and another. Pretty soon, Tanner had been caught up in a web of hate and crime and probably hadn't been able to see any way out.

Tyler knew Cass well enough to recognize that he considered Tanner one of his men now. That meant even if Ty hadn't felt the same way, Tanner would now be under the protection of Cass and the rest of the men at the ranch. They would all work to do what needed to be done in order to protect the young man—as long as he continued to step up and take responsibility for his actions. That included finding a way to stop Old Man Trip and Tanner's asshole brother, T-bone.

He'd just finished assembling the casserole when he heard voices in the hall.

"This fucking sucks. The boy is going to be overwhelmed with guilt," Chance said.

"Yep."

Tyler heard the strain in Cass's voice, even in that clipped one-word answer. They stepped into the kitchen as Cass continued, "Not much we can do about that except go forward like we told him we would. I was going to wait until eight before I called the attorneys, but I'm thinking maybe I should go ahead and call Cade's cell phone. This has the potential to blow up in a hurry."

"What's happened?" Ty asked.

Cass blinked over at him before crossing the room and folding Tyler into a hug. "Sorry, babe," his cowboy said. "I nearly forgot the most important thing." Cass cupped Ty's cheeks in his rough, callused hands and brought their mouths together. His tongue pressed in, slid against Ty's, a slick, wet reminder of all the wicked pleasures it could bring. Ty moaned into Cass's mouth.

After several long moments of nearly mind-numbing kisses, Chance cleared his throat. "Unless you two need a few more minutes alone, let's catch Ty up on what he missed. Or, I suppose, if you're going to be a while, I could go find Bryan…I did leave in rather a hurry this morning."

Cass slowly drew back, his teeth dragging over Ty's lower lip before he finally released him. "Love you," he whispered.

"Love you too, cowboy." Ty smiled up at his partner. "Now, why don't you tell me why Chance's panties are in a twist."

Cass gave a little snort and Chance laughed softly while he poured himself another cup of coffee from the percolator.

"That coffee's been cooking all morning. It'll put hair on your chest," Ty said.

"Too late," Chance said. "As to what happened? Tanner got a phone call about half an hour ago. His brother and father were involved in a motor vehicle versus tractor-trailer accident on I-40, near Seligman. T-bone was killed outright and Trip was medivaced to Flagstaff. It sounds like it's touch and go, so Tanner and Park took off for the hospital."

"Shit. Are you sure? You don't think Tanner is going to run, do you?" Ty asked.

Cass barked a short laugh. "Hell, if he is running, then it's because Chance gave him the suggestion."

Tyler looked from his lover to Chance and saw they were both smiling. "What am I missing?"

"Actually, I did tell him going into hiding was one option. Tanner stepped up, though. He said he wouldn't run. He agreed to disclose what he knows about his father and what's been going on surrounding the Trip-T. Cass was going to put him in touch with the Flagstaff attorneys first, so they could negotiate a deal that will hopefully keep Tanner out of jail and put the rest of the bastards behind bars."

Tyler frowned a little as he went to the stove to follow Chance's example and poured another cup of coffee. "Are we sure the call was genuine?"

"He was standing next to me when he took it. I saw the hospital name on the caller ID. He dialed the number back and got the hospital switchboard. But, yeah—the timing seemed too damned cute to me too. I called a friend in Flag who is going to double check"—he glanced at the clock—"but it might take a while…"

Sipping his coffee, Ty thought the situation over. It had been a few years since he'd worked as a Navy SEAL, but some lessons were so deeply ingrained they were impossible to ignore. The situation between the Trip-T and the WSR qualified as a hostile action by anyone's definition. They'd been attacked, there was confirmation of a planned takeover, and the intention to harm Cass and his ranch clear. Assess and adjust.

"If this so-called general or T-bone have a clue Tanner could be at the WSR, they won't stop at anything to shut him up," Ty said.

"What are you thinking?" Cass asked.

"I think Tanner is a liability they can't afford."

"I agree. Let me do what I should have done in the first place. The Highway Patrol will be able to confirm an accident on I-40." Chance pulled his cell phone from his holster and turned away.

"Cass, even if the call is legit...I think I should to go to Flag. Someone needs to be with him for a day or two. At least until he talks to Cade and Carter and they can put him in contact with whichever law enforcement agency takes this on. He's going to be in danger—"

"Fuck," Chance exploded. He clipped his phone back in place. "There's no accident. It's a fucking setup. I'm going after them, Cass. They're only ten minutes or so ahead of me, and I can go a hell of a lot faster in one of our trucks—"

"Quit talking, let's go," Ty interrupted. "Cass, you try and call Tanner on his cell. He might still be close enough to have reception. Keep calling, because as soon as they get close enough to the highway—"

"Goddammit, Ty, you don't need—"

"Cass, we don't need to cover old ground. You know I'm the best man for this. Now, you call Chad and ask him to come watch the casserole." Ty leaned in and kissed Cass into a sputtering silence. "It's going to be okay. You take care of things here, and Chance and I will get Tanner someplace safe."

"I agree," Chance said. "The sooner he's talking to the feds, the safer everyone's going to be. Cass—call Holden. Set up some more security. And don't worry about Ty, he's right. You know he's the best. We'll call as soon as we know something."

****

Starting with the assumption that Tanner was at the WSR and his phone was functional was a risk worth taking. If he was wrong, it would only delay any alternative plans by a few hours, but he needed to rule out the worst-case scenario before he tried anything else. T-bone's biggest concern had been whether his brother still had his cellphone, but since there'd been no sign of it at the campsite, the odds were on his side that Tanner had it clipped to his hip as usual when he'd crawled away from the attack.

If his brother decided to grow a conscience and talk, the damage he could do to their cause was nearly incalculable, and he had to be stopped at all costs. He'd been tempted to draw him to the Trip-T, then dispose of the body somewhere on their thousands of acres. It wasn't likely anyone official would come searching, but there was no sense leaving a trail to their door.

No, it was far better to leave the mess at the doorstep of the man responsible for this whole situation. Cass Cartwright. It wouldn't matter if the WSR mustered a dozen witnesses to say Tanner was there voluntarily. It was damned hard to explain a dead body on your ranch. Particularly if there was evidence that said body belonged to the man responsible for sabotaging your ranch to the tune of tens of thousands of dollars.

After working through the night to meld a sufficient amount of charge with his radio-activated device, he'd scraped away enough dirt to set the bomb in the ideal location. There was just no way to make the turn at the junction between the WSR and the state road that led to I-40 without slowing down. He wasn't particularly worried about leaving trace evidence of a bomb, since whichever vehicle Tanner was in was going to burn hot enough to show Tanner had been carrying the explosives himself.

The call was easy to arrange. One of the general's faithful worked at the Flag hospital, and he had been more than happy to place the call. Scripting the fake situation hadn't been hard either. Tanner was a sap. No matter what information he knew about their father, his brother would always come if he thought the old man was in danger. When the hospital employee called a little while ago to say he'd been successful in contacting Tanner with the news, T-bone got into position. Now his suspicions were confirmed. Tanner was alive. *Fuck—Bingo—Fuck.*

A plus B usually equaled C. Emergency call to Tanner plus a vehicle leaving the WSR less than an hour later equaled Tanner leaving the relative safety of the queers. The very predictability of ranch life meant that this early in the morning, the hands would be busy with feeding, mucking out stalls, or on their way to the distant paddocks and fence lines. The overwhelming odds were that Tanner would be inside the truck. If not? Well, the world would be better off without one of the faggots, and anything to cause more problems for Cartwright was all good.

T-bone lay prone and watched through the field glasses as a piece of shit hippie van approached. He'd been expecting one of the WSR ranch trucks, maybe with Cartwright or one of the others along for the ride. Apparently, Tanner wasn't to be trusted with one of their work vehicles, though. Whatever. It would still burn.

The ancient orange and white van slowed to approach the turn and the point of detonation. T-bone's finger hovered over the trigger switch. "Come on…closer. Closer…"

The view through the front windshield of the van made him want to vomit. His brother was there all right. Along with some long-haired freak. The two men looked be having some sort of argument—like some kind of a goddamn couple. Tanner said something to the driver just as T-bone closed the switch. As if in slow motion, then van seemed to crawl to a stop, the other man turned to face Tanner, then the earth around them exploded. The front wheels lifted into the air as the van went nearly airborne, spun around, then crashed to the ground. Smoke billowed and dirt and stones rained down. It was funny how plans could change in a flash of a fireball, T-bone thought.

****

Ty held on to the doorframe as Chance rocketed them over the familiar WSR ranch road at a speed that had his bones rattling. By mutual agreement, they'd decided to run the truck dark. In the pale pre-dawn light, hitting a stray coyote at this speed could cause a big problem, so Ty kept up a continuous scan of the landscape ahead.

"It's going to be here on the ranch or on Ranch Road Seven," Chance said for the third time.

"Yep. The intersect is the most likely place…" Ty agreed again. "If we have to stop, you take left, I got right. Shoot to kill, no unnecessary chances."

"I got it. You think it will be more than one? Because I have a sense this T-bone character might be acting on his own."

"He probably is, but if Tanner's been missing for three days and they caught on right away—that's a hell of a long time to plan or bring in reinforcements." Ty braced his other hand on the dash as they hit a deep rut.

Chance grunted. "Yeah. I wish to fuck we had a clue what we're facing. Could be a sniper rifle or an explosive device."

"Hell, it could be another damn vehicle. If they have a heavy truck, they could do a lot of damage with a sideswipe and force Tanner off the road. Depends on if they want him alive for questioning first."

"We're less than a mile from the turn off."

"Yep. I think I see them," he said. "Caught a quick flash of something."

"Yes, that's gotta be them," Chance agreed and stepped on the accelerator. "Should I flash the lights?"

Before Ty could answer, there was a bright flash on the road in front of them, then the lights from the van danced crazily before blinking out.

"I vote explosives," Chance muttered as he pressed the accelerator to close the quarter mile distance.

"Doesn't mean there isn't still someone with a gun. I have a feeling the general would want to know for certain whether Tanner already talked to us. Stop here long enough to let me out." Scanning the area, Ty came to a quick decision.

"I'll circle around to come up from behind anyone who might be waiting to ambush. You head to the crash but keep the truck…and yourself on this side of the van. If you can get them inside the van, take off. Do not wait for me." He opened the door and jumped down.

"Bullshit. Cass would—"

"Don't fucking argue, just go. I don't want to give away that someone might be out here on foot." Without waiting for any further argument, Ty quietly closed the truck door and took off at a light jog, the knife in his hand a comfortable friend.

Chapter Ten

One second Tanner was looking at Park, trying to sort through his surprising words, the next second he was jerked and tumbled as gravity seemed to lose all control. Park's arm hit him in the chest, as if he tried to hold Tanner in place, then he lost his sense of up and down. The seat belt cut into his stomach and gripped him across his chest, then his head shot forward, before his neck snapped to the left, shooting pain through his arm that burned all the way up to the base of his skull. Tanner might have been screaming, but the screech of metal drowned all other sounds. Everything seemed to be going in slow motion, yet Tanner couldn't make his arms move fast enough to protect Park as his head whipped forward and smacked into the steering wheel. With a sickening thud, the van slammed into the ground and finally shuddered to a stop.

He blinked rapidly, surprised to realize he was still conscious. The smell of gasoline conjured visions of every Fast and Furious movie to dance in front of his eyes, and he almost held his breath waiting for the as-seen-on-the-screen moment when the van would burst into a dramatic fireball.

Jesus Christ, what am I thinking? He frantically worked at the seat belt latch, propping himself against the dash which now seemed to be on the floor, if his sense of up and down had returned. The buckle came loose with a clatter and he tumbled forward.

"Park?" He hoped he was whispering the question, but there was so much ringing in his ears he couldn't be sure. He pressed two fingers to his lover's neck and found a steady, if elevated, pulse rate. Couldn't blame him for that, Tanner's heart was racing too.

"Come on, Park. We have to get out of here," he said, even as he started tugging at the other man's buckle to no avail. The sense of urgency was only half spurred by thoughts of fire. The other very real fear came from his certainty that this had been no accident.

This fucking set up had T-bone's name all over it. He'd been a stupid fool to fall for that call. Despite the caller ID, despite the switchboard, his brother had managed to cut through Tanner's defenses by going after his biggest weakness. *Their father.* Because no matter how much he wished he didn't, Tanner still craved the older man's approval. It was stupid and something that would never...*could* never happen.

Even if he hadn't already committed to help put his dad behind bars, Tanner had crossed that invisible line he'd drawn for himself. It was a world of difference between knowing you were gay and actually *being* gay.

Acting gay?

Whatever you wanted to call what he and Park did last night.

Sex? Lovers? Friends?

God, his thoughts were all over the place. He needed to think. No, goddammit. He needed to move.

His brother was out there somewhere, and Tanner needed to get Park to safety. That triggered a thought. He could call for help. He patted his hip, finding only a belt where his phone should have been clipped. There was no telling where the small instrument would have landed, so after a cursory look around, he quit and went back to the problem of freeing Park from his seat belt. In an ideal world, he'd help to support Park in place until help arrived to avoid causing further injury from movement. This wasn't that world. He needed to get Park to safety, right the fuck now.

Aware that his brain was not functioning normally, Tanner clamped down on his unruly thoughts and focused on the belt. Switching from trying to use his numb right hand, he squeezed at the latch with his left and was relieved when he felt the mechanism release.

Park's body slumped forward slightly before sliding toward the van's center console. *Shit.* He hadn't thought this through. Propping Park with one hand, Tanner forced his numb arm into motion and tucked his hand over the handle. Pushing all thoughts of pain aside, he pulled up, then pried, the door open. The distinctive screech of metal against metal was loud—signaling the van held survivors capable of escape. *Fuck.*

Fueled by desperation, Tanner twisted and pulled on Park until he was clear of the console and mostly laying across the passenger seat. With each effort to bring Park forward, Tanner moved back, until he was standing outside the mangled van, his breath coming in loud gasps. Wrapping his arms around Park's shoulders and under his thighs, Tanner grunted with effort as he lifted the smaller man from the seat, then turned away from the van. The smell of gas was strong enough to taste, removing any choice from his actions.

T-bone would be operating under the get-in-get-out rule. Do as much damage as possible then retreat before any possibility of discovery. Killing or capturing Tanner would be his primary objective, and there was no way he would risk leaving before that mission was accomplished. Gas was spilling, raising the possibility that fire was imminent. Leaving Park protected by the hulking metal carcass of his van was not an option. He needed to get Park away from the vehicle, leave him alone on the ground, while Tanner drew Tim's attention in the opposite direction. With a mental eye roll, he acknowledged the futility of the plan, but it was the best he had.

The van catching fire would be the best-case scenario, because then all he needed to do was wait for the blaze to be spotted and survive fifteen or twenty minutes with his psychopath brother stalking him—oh and never mind that baby bro would be armed.

Tanner cursed the rapidly lightening sky, shifted Park in his arms, and resisted looking toward the tree line on the other side of the Ranch Road Seven junction. He didn't need to look in order to know that was where Tim would have been watching for their vehicle. Turning in the general direction from which they'd come, he blinked rapidly, trying to sort through anything to explain the rapid approach of a king-cab, no headlights, no running lights, a shadow behind the wheel. With barely enough time to react, the truck spun toward him in a hailstorm of pebbles and he twisted away to protect Park from further injury. The door swung open and Chance jumped out, his mouth moving.

"Get in, get in, get in," he chanted, his voice a harsh whisper, as if his arrival would be a secret. He opened the rear door of the big truck and Tanner staggered forward. Together, the two of them maneuvered Park into the backseat. The truck lurched to the left a second before the sound of a rifle shot reached their ears, followed by the realization that one of the tires had just been shot out.

"Fuck," Chance shouted, apparently no longer concerned with keeping quiet. "Get in."

Another shot rang out, this one embedding itself in the front of the truck. A hiss of steam and the sweet smell of radiator fluid mingled with the odor of gas. They were ducks in a shooting gallery.

"Get Park the fuck out of here," Tanner said. "I'll draw his fire."

"No, wait, Ty's—"

"Go before the fucking van explodes, goddammit," Tanner shouted. Without waiting for an argument, he circled around the van, then ran toward the closest clump of juniper trees. Knowing he was backlit by the approaching sunrise, and expecting T-bone to be watching, Tanner zigged then zagged, throwing in a little unnecessary arm movement just to make sure he caught his brother's attention. Fifteen feet from his goal, the earth at his feet exploded, followed by the rifle crack. Stones bit into his skin, and Tanner dove toward the protection of the tree.

"Oh fuck."

****

Refusing to allow himself to be distracted or discouraged by the arrival of a WSR ranch truck, T-bone reassessed the situation. The two men at the truck, although tempting, were not his main target. If he failed to kill Tanner, everything else was pointless. That didn't mean he couldn't use the other men to his advantage. Clearly Tanner had some attachment to them since he was deliberately drawing fire in the opposite direction. Unfortunately, time was at a premium as someone would no doubt have already called to the ranch or 9-1-1. Either way, T-bone had less than a ten-minute window that he could count on before the possibility of help arrived. Time was not on his side.

"Daddy wants to talk to you, Tanner. If you come over here, I'll leave the other two alone," T-bone called softly.

"Fuck you."

"I think I'll leave that to the fags. If you want them to live, you better come with me."

"Never going to happen, Timothy. Get out of here while you can."

Apparently big brother thought he stood a chance. Wrong. Tanner never had been very good at seeing what was right under his nose. Despite how dense he could be, no doubt he'd finally figured out that his goals and T-bone's were mutually exclusive. On such a short timeline, there was no sense in dragging things out. T-bone needed to get closer. He fired another shot toward the truck, and despite the bad angle from being on the wrong side of the van, he caught an edge of the windshield. The fact that nobody fired back at him, probably meant they were unarmed. What a bunch of idiots. Or maybe the long-haired one was so badly injured the other man was distracted. Either way, he'd incapacitated the truck, and he would deal with them once Tanner was out of the way.

Moving farther from where he'd parked his own truck behind a grove of juniper, T-bone began to track toward the road. There was still plenty of cover and obviously Tanner was also unarmed or he'd already have returned fire.

As the sun crested the horizon, the bright light was blinding, forcing T-bone to lower the bill of his ball cap. It might hamper his range of vision a bit, but his target was straight in front of him. As if he'd heard the thought, Tanner stuck his head out from behind the ancient tree and T-bone fired. Bark exploded from the edge of the broad trunk, but the bullet failed to find its target. He wasn't going to be able to shoot Tanner through the tree, but once he got close enough, he'd no doubt be able to chase Tanner out from behind his wall of protection.

Another quick glance toward the rapidly rising sun set his heart rate racing. Time was his enemy here. Never taking his gaze from his target, T-bone left the relative shelter of one grove of trees and headed to the next, bringing him closer to the road—to his target. Closer to finishing this mess.

****

Circling around so that he was positioned behind T-bone was no problem for Tyler. The man only had eyes for what was directly in front of him, without any awareness that he'd left himself wide open to attack. Ty moved closer, mirroring the other man's steps, keeping to the relative cover of the larger juniper trees.

In this part of Arizona, the oldest of the trees stood in circles of threes and fours, and a careful search at the base of these clusters would often yield ancient Native American artifacts. Just as they'd provided shelter hundreds of years ago, they continue to provide shelter today, and Ty hoped that Tanner was smart enough to stay behind the tree he'd chosen as his shield. T-bone's rifle wouldn't be able to penetrate the thick trunk.

The sun settled above the horizon, turning T-bone into a glowing temptation of a target. Ty was careful to tightly clamp down on any fantasy of using the gun tucked into the waistband of his jeans to just shoot the bastard in the back. Easy, but not particularly satisfying. The preferable solution would be to capture the asswipe and make him accountable to the system. They wanted to bring down the whole network, not have the trail end here at the WSR, only to sprout somewhere else. In order for that to happen, Tanner needed to survive, but unfortunately, so did his brother.

Silently closing the gap between them, Ty maneuvered further to the left, knowing T-bone would be focused on Tanner first and consider the others secondary targets. Ten more feet…eight…

He was just reaching for his gun when T-bone stepped to the left, his foot slipping on the granite and sandstone, spinning him around as he stumbled to one knee. His rifle wavered for a second as he caught himself, then came down steady to point at Ty's chest, even as he blinked in surprise to find someone behind him.

Apparently recovering quickly, T-bone glanced at Ty's knife hand, lowered the barrel of his weapon slightly, and grinned. "Seriously? You brought a knife to a gunfight?" He laughed at his own joke. "You are exactly what I need to make sure Tanner sees things my way. Get your ass over here." He gestured with the rifle to indicate he wanted Ty to come around in front of him.

"Put the gun down, Tim," Ty said, deliberately using the man's given name. Getting his first up close and personal of the infamous T-bone Triplett dropped a lot of things into perspective. "You don't stand a chance of getting out of here. Police are already on their way, and they know it's you they're looking for."

"Fuck you. You have no idea who you're messing with. Gonna kill you and your faggot friends if you don't move your goddamn pansy-ass over here." His eyes narrowed, and his mouth was a thin, angry line.

"Better think again, Tim." Ty barely resisted rolling his eyes. He could crush the little bastard with one hand and leave his best weapon hanging by his side. This wasn't a contest in anyone's book. T-bone was barely a man in Ty's eyes, nothing more than a punk kid who'd turned bullying into murder. All of his macho bullshit homophobic posturing was probably for effect.

The easy psychobabble answer was to guess he was a closet case. Smaller than his older brother, with delicate features and a slender build, there wasn't any doubt in Ty's mind he would at least have been hit on once or twice in his life. Given his upbringing, Tim would have freaked out. But there was no amount of pop psychology to excuse years of abuse or murder or the association with a megalomaniac set on creating his own nation. No matter how you looked at it, Tim Triplett deserved to spend his life behind bars, not get the easy way out with a quick death.

Keeping his anger in check, Ty tried again. "I'd prefer to keep you alive, but I *will* kill you if you don't drop your weapon."

"Fucker. Think you could? You and what army?"

As if in slow motion, Ty saw the barrel of the weapon raise, the slight shift of finger inside the trigger guard, and the cold, flat look of deadly intent. *Well—shit.*

Feinting left, lunging right, he threw his knife while still mid-jump. The rifle clattered to the dirt as T-bone went over onto his side, his hand clutching at the hilt of the knife, the blade buried just under his collarbone.

Ty continued his roll. Coming back up on his feet, he closed the three steps necessary to recover the rifle. Lowering the barrel to a few inches above the gasping Tim's face, he made sure he had the young man's attention. "Don't need an army—I'm Navy-trained."

Chapter Eleven

Two weeks later

Park turned the dough he was working with into a lightly oiled bowl and draped a clean dishtowel over the top. After washing his hands, he put the bowl on a shelf in the warmer to rise, automatically glancing at the clock. Still three hours before the crack of dawn. He'd been awake for nearly two hours already—which explained the dough—but it was still too early to start packing.

"What are you doing in my kitchen?" Ty asked, causing Park to jump.

"Cooking something to eat." Park wasn't sure why he bothered to answer. Neither the question, nor his response had changed for the last two weeks. Of course, Park didn't usually show up at oh-dark-thirty—as Ty would say—so maybe there *was* a reason to ask, after all, he conceded.

Ty stood for a minute, hands on his hips as his gaze traveled over the dusting of flour on the stainless work station, then shifted to the dirty dishes in the sink. Park's already frayed temper snapped. "I'll have them out of your way in a minute," he ground out between clenched teeth.

Without replying, Ty headed straight for the stove. Park had spent enough time in the kitchen to know Ty's usual custom was to start a pot of coffee on the stove, before he did anything else. Hoping to avoid any conflict, Park had already taken care of that little detail.

"Hmm...you made coffee?"

"Yes. Look, I'm sorry. I know I'm in your space. Give me a minute to wash these up, then I'll be out of your way."

Ty poured a large mug of coffee, flipped the switch on the industrial-sized coffee urn to start the brew for everyone else, then leaned his hips against the counter and studied Park over the rim of his cup.

Park ran a sink full of hot water and pretended he didn't notice the big cook staring daggers.

"Kind of hard to get out of my way when you have dough rising in my proof oven. What's in the bowl?"

"Pumpkin cinnamon rolls. I can wait to roll them out until you're finished with whatever you have planned."

"How many did you make?"

"Two dozen. I know that's not enough, but I thought you could..." Park rolled his eyes. "Look, I'm sorry. I should have asked first."

"Two dozen, huh? That's enough for half the men. Let's double the batch. Where's the recipe?"

"Oh, I uh…" Park glanced around the kitchen, looking for a way out of this awkward conversation.

Ty sighed. "Let me guess…you don't measure?"

Unable to hide his grin, Park shook his head. "If you want, I'll make a second batch over here out of your way, and you can go ahead with whatever you had planned."

"Nah, I usually just have coffee and biscuits or rolls for the men before the first round of chores. I think I'll sit here with my coffee and watch you."

"Oh, uh—"

When Ty refilled his coffee and pulled up a stool, Park realized the man was serious. Returning to the pantry, he pulled out the bag of baking ingredients he'd purchased when they'd been in Kingman, after Manny—one of the longtime Willow Springs ranch hands—had taken him to the ER. *After Tanner disappeared with the men in black.*

"You haven't heard from Tanner, have you?" Ty asked, as if following his thoughts.

"No. No real reason to, I suppose. I heard from the car dealer in Kingman, though. They found me another van. It's a later model, but I think it will be fine. They are fitting it with the updated safety belts and doing some engine work, but I can pick it up on Monday."

"I'll take you to get it," Ty offered. "I need supplies, anyway. What kind of flour is that?" he asked as Park scooped several cups into a mixing bowl."

"Organic whole wheat pastry."

"Okay, I'll make sure to get you some more."

"Oh—thanks, but there's no need really. I'm going to head out as soon as I get my van."

"Head out? You're not going to wait for Tanner?" Ty frowned.

Park sighed, but didn't respond right away. He added the rest of the dry ingredients to the bowl and set it aside. He looked at Ty, but other than a politely interested expression, the big cook still didn't speak— just left that thought hanging between them.

Tanner. The biggest regret of my life. Oh, not being with him, that had been...perfect. But it had been a mistake. Not something the closeted cowboy had been ready for, and definitely not something Park should have pushed while so many things in Tanner's life had been in turmoil. He could have—should have—waited, given everything he'd known about Tanner's circumstances growing up.

Grabbing a wooden spoon, he attacked the ingredients, sending up a small cloud of flour. He flicked a glance toward Ty and thought he caught a hint of a smile, but the other man stared into his cup. *And waited.*

Ignoring Ty, Park went back to thinking about Tanner. He always seemed to get back to that. He'd tried many times over the last two weeks to imagine a life that included a brother who hated you enough to try to kill you. Not just once but twice. A sick, homophobic father. To watch your life's dream be destroyed and still try for the approval all children needed to grow up healthy and strong.

Maybe if he'd kept his hormones in check, then Tanner would have called to tell him he was okay. Would have realized, above everything else, that Park wanted him as a friend—was someone safe.

Park turned the dough onto the floured surface and punched it a little harder than was necessary before he started to form the ball. His decision cemented and the need to make it more real through sharing made him look up to meet the big cook's steady gaze. "Look, Ty, I don't belong here, and there's just no real reason for me to stay. Tanner isn't coming back, and even if he did…there's nothing between—"

"Okay, so the dough is made. You let it rise until double? Right?" Ty interrupted.

Jerked back to thinking about his pumpkin rolls, Park agreed. "Yes, then roll it out, spread the pumpkin mixture, rise again. Bake as usual."

Ty pushed to his feet. "Okay, I can handle that. Why don't you go take a shower?" He crossed to the stove to refill his coffee, then turned to face Park.

Park stared back at Ty, his mouth opened and closed repeatedly as he thought of, then discarded, several retorts. "Shower?" he finally said.

"Yeah, you know, hot water, soap, shampoo. You probably should put that shit on your eyes, too. Jesus, Park, you don't normally strike me as this stupid."

Heat rushed to his face, and Park straightened his shoulders. "What the—just because I was in your kitchen doesn't mean—" He broke off when he realized Ty was fighting a smile.

"What's going on, Ty?"

Ty looked at the clock, then back at Park. "Chance has been in Flag the last two days, right? He and Tanner are on their way here, right now. You've got about thirty minutes. Go on, get cleaned up."

Thoughts raced through his mind and tried to come out in a jumble of words. "But— I don't think— What if he—"

"Park, he's coming here. Let that be enough, for now."

****

As was his custom when riding shotgun in the dark, Tanner kept a lookout as they traveled through elk and deer country along the I-40 corridor. It would suck to have a vehicle versus animal accident when he was so close to freedom. Not that he was exactly finished with his obligations, but after two long weeks, the federal prosecutor agreed with the investigators that Tanner could be released provided they were assured he would return to testify. Until then, charges would hang over his head and Cass

Cartwright would be out a chunk of money if Tanner failed to appear. That wasn't going to happen. There were many debts that needed to be paid.

The truck slowed as they approached the intersection at Ranch Road Seven and the WSR. Chance glanced over at him and Tanner met his gaze. "You okay?"

"Yeah. I'm kind of glad it's dark right now, though. I don't really need any more reminders of the accident. Are you sure Park's okay?"

"I'm sure. Well, unless Ty has killed him by now."

"Ty? Why would Ty try to kill Park?"

"Oh, I don't know. It might have something to do with his vegan requirements and Ty's kitchen."

"Oh yeah. I kind of forgot Park was vegan. We never got around to discussing food." Tanner's face heated, and he was grateful there was still so much time left before sunrise.

Chance snorted. "No, I don't suppose you did. So why didn't you call him? He's been moping around the WSR ever since we returned from the hospital that day. He wanted to track you down, but had to settle for a trip to the health food store instead."

Tanner laughed. "Well, I suppose if he was well enough to shop for food after the accident, then he really is okay, isn't he?" Despite the laugh, he could still hear the anxiety in his voice.

The aftermath of the accident had been terrible. While he'd held Park, trying to wake him with whispers and stolen kisses, Ty had dragged T-bone to the road. His brother had been bleeding and cussing at Ty, calling them all faggots and worse. It had been humiliating, and yet, he hadn't pulled away from Park—despite knowing his brother could see him, would get word to their father. It was a defining and liberating moment he would never forget.

Less than twenty minutes later, Cass and Manny had arrived, each bringing a ranch truck. Chance had put a still groggy but finally conscious Park into a seat belt and placed Manny in charge of getting him to Kingman for medical treatment. After that, Tanner's life really hadn't been his own, because Chance's pal from the FBI had shown up and escorted him to the Mohave County Courthouse.

For the last two weeks, it had been one government office after another, sworn testimony, affidavits, and lawyers. Thank God for Cass's attorneys, Cade and Carter. One of them had been by his side each step of the way. For now, he was officially in a standby status until the next round of questioning began.

"Yes, Tanner, Park really is okay. Care to tell me why you decided not to call him once you got the all clear for outside contact?" Chance asked.

Tanner chewed on his lip for a minute. "Park is different from anyone I ever met," he said at last.

"No shit. And that means…" Chance said.

The silence stretched for several miles. The reasons made sense in his head, but they had another fifteen minutes before they reached the ranch house, and he wasn't sure that was enough time to make Chance understand.

"I don't mean that Park is different in a bad way. He's a good man. He worked helping kids in trouble. He helped Chad get out of that mess with the school in Flagstaff. He helped me," he said on a near whisper.

"So why shut him out...or— Tanner, is there some kind of worthiness issue going on here? Because I'm pretty damned sure Park would call bullshit."

"I know he would, and that's the problem, isn't it? You've spent days with me Chance...and with the investigators. You know better than anyone how fucked up I am. Park deserves—"

"Don't fucking say it." Chance's voice rang out, and he pointed at Tanner. "Don't you goddamn say it. You bet your ass I think you fucked up. But you caught a raw deal in the parenting department, too. The point isn't what you did in the past—hell, half the feds in Arizona are working out what to do about your past."

Chance gripped the wheel with both hands, and the truck shot forward, bumping and rattling Tanner's teeth. "You stepped up now, and that counts for more. You've got Cass on your side, because he believes in you. Hell—do you know how many hours I've spent on the phone talking to one agency or another? How much driving back and forth? Do you think I would have done any of that if I didn't think you were worth it?"

Tanner blinked, stunned into silence by Chance's outburst. "I, uh—"

"Look," Chance said on a sigh. "Bryan…my partner…I almost lost him." Chance swallowed hard. "I've been digging through the evidence that my pal Eli could let me see. We'll never prove it, but I know T-bone was involved in his kidnapping. You're helping to put that prick behind bars. That puts you on the right side of this mess, Tanner. Don't think you have all the answers here, because you don't. Park gets to make his own decisions."

Chapter Twelve

With his head in his hands, Tanner sat on the bed in Park's room—the room they'd shared for a single night—and listened to the spray of water from behind the closed door. Park was in the shower, unaware of Tanner's presence. According to Ty, Park knew his arrival was imminent and had raced off to dress for the day. That was a damned shame. A naked Park was just what he needed right now. Just what he'd been dreaming of the past two weeks. Which had been pretty awkward, given the number of different men and women who had been traipsing through his various hotel rooms. Kingman. Flagstaff. Phoenix.

Of course that had been all business. This was…well, he didn't know what it was. He didn't know what he wanted it to be, either, but with Chance's words still echoing in his head, he realized everything wasn't up to him.

Park would have a lot to say about what happened next. Given the breadth and depth of Tanner's crimes, a man of Park's intelligence would have only one real choice. Tanner was likely to end up out in the kitchen in twenty minutes, asking for a room of his own. Which went a long way to explaining why he hadn't contacted Park by phone when he'd been given the all clear two days ago. He just hadn't wanted to be told no over the phone.

Now that he was here, with nothing but a door separating them, Tanner wasn't sure he could bear the rejection in person any better.

Then the door to the bathroom opened, and Tanner lifted his head to meet the steady blue-gray gaze that haunted his days and nights. Everything that had been bubbling inside Tanner slowed down, and he swore it felt like he and Park were the only two people in the world. How could that be? How could this one man be the beginning, the end, everything?

"Kismet?" Park said, as if he somehow knew what Tanner had been thinking.

Tanner was off the bed and folding Park in his arms, their mouths meeting in a searing kiss. Park met the force of Tanner's kiss and returned it with an edge of rawness, as though they were on the same battlefield of need.

"God," Park murmured. "I wasn't sure...I thought you didn't..."

"Let me..." Tanner slowly turned them, as if they were slow dancing, then pressed the palm of his hand on Park's belly and edged him back to the mattress.

As soon as the backs of his knees bumped, Park flopped onto his back and Tanner followed him over, crawled right on top of Park's thinner body and settled between Park's legs. Careful to keep just enough of his own weight supported so he didn't crush the smaller man, Tanner bracketed Park's head with his arms and looked into his beautiful eyes, the warmth from them stealing right into Tanner's terrified heart.

"I don't have any right to be here with you, but there isn't anywhere else I want to be…" Tanner said. He dipped down as the words escaped and captured Park's mouth in a slow, easy kiss.

At the first touch of their lips, Park moaned and his entire body relaxed, as if welcoming Tanner's weight. From the moment he'd met this man, Tanner had been filled with a need, with desire like he'd never known. In his dreams, while he was awake, it didn't seem to matter, his body hungered.

Park slid his fingers up Tanner's forearm, over his shoulders, a constant motion, although whether to soothe or just keep them anchored together, Tanner didn't know. Didn't care. He just didn't want the touching to stop.

"You said I could explore…next time," he whispered against Park's kiss-swollen lips.

"Yes…no…wait." Park's voice was raspy, and he blinked rapidly, as if trying to focus on the words.

"No?" Tanner said, moving his lips to Park's neck, nuzzling against the moist warm skin. "You want me to stop?"

"No…yes…oh shit. Wait a minute, Tanner."

Realizing Park was serious, Tanner stopped the kisses and sat up on his haunches, his heart thundering and not in a good way. *Oh shit, this is it.* Park was going to ask him to leave. Yeah, the man was sexually aroused, the head of his cock peeking out from the bath towel, but sex wasn't the issue…

"I'm sorry—" Tanner started, but Park cut him off.

"You should be…naked, too," Park said, a lazy grin lighting his face.

A weight lifted from his heart and Tanner jumped from the bed. "Yes, you're right. I should be naked. His words were lost as he grabbed the hem of his tee shirt and pulled it over his head before tossing it aside. The tip of Park's tongue darted out to moisten his lips as Tanner unfastened the top button on his jeans. As much as he wanted to feel that hot mouth on his cock, there were other things he wanted more. Things he needed more. Lowering the zipper, he pushed down the heavy denim and stepped clear of his clothes.

"Better?" he asked as Park's hot gaze raked down his body.

"Much. Now get back down here… *Mi casa es su casa*… God, please I don't even know what I'm saying—just touch me," Park begged.

Needing no further invitation, Tanner crawled back between Park's legs, going straight for the tempting flat disc of a nipple. He swiped his tongue over the slightly raised flesh, then latched on, alternately sucking and scraping his teeth over the tiny nub. Park arched into the touch, his hands forcing Tanner's face harder against his chest.

"More."

Tanner shifted his attention to the other nipple, while Park continued to hold his head tightly and make throaty little murmurs of encouragement that were sexy as hell. Park's hips moved rhythmically, stabbing at Tanner's stomach, leaving smears of pre-cum on his skin.

Looking up at Park through half-closed lids, he kissed his way down the flat abs, pausing to dip his tongue into the indent of his belly button, before daring to go lower. "Want to taste you, Park."

"Oh yes, please. Make me come with your mouth. I'll warn you before I shoot, honey."

"Yes." An undeniable longing burned inside Tanner, his need for this man's cock engulfed him in flames, threatening to consume him whole. The noise that escaped was more growl than moan, and he swiped his tongue over the broad crown for his first taste of another man's cock. Tentatively at first, he licked and kissed, amazed at both the similarities and the differences between them. Like the rest of him, Park's cock was long and slender, with a definite curve to the left. He wanted to swallow every bit of the man down.

Wrapping his lips around the mushroom-shaped head, Tanner's mouth was full of hot, throbbing dick. The clean, musky scent of man invaded his nostrils and slipped right into his bloodstream, to course through his body, pump through his heart.

A harsh, needful noise from Park had Tanner bobbing up and down, hungry for every taste he could get. He reached between Park's thighs and massaged his tight, cum-filled balls, alternating between rolling and tugging on the lightly furred sac.

Park groaned, his lids sliding closed as Tanner continued to touch and taste his cock and balls. Relaxing his jaw, Tanner took more of Park's length, gratified when Park squirmed, his legs falling open even farther as Tanner sucked him down. He wasn't taking Park as deep as he should, but he didn't want to gag and ruin the moment.

Park's inability to remain still or even relatively quiet heated Tanner's desire to let everything loose with this man—to see just how crazy he could make his…lover. Releasing Park's balls, he gripped his hips with both hands, his fingers digging in to the pale flesh hard enough he was afraid he'd leave bruises. Then he half-hoped he would because the thought of marking Park brought a growl of possessiveness from somewhere deep inside.

"Oh yeah… Holy hell." Park bucked his hips at Tanner's face. "So…" He twisted his fist into the sheets. "So fucking close. Pull back. Finish me with your hand, honey."

At those words, Tanner grew impossibly harder. His cock and ass pulsed with the need to come but he ignored the desire to touch himself, not finished exploring the man before him. He made his tongue flat and licked along the underside of Park's cock, sliding the smooth cap against the roof of his mouth. Pre-come leaked, giving more hints of the taste trapped in Park's balls. Using plenty of spit and carefully breathing through his nose, Tanner worked until he got Park to the back of his mouth. Then he kept right on going, pushing the mushroom head further down his throat. And then a little bit more. When he couldn't take any more, Tanner swallowed around the long shaft.

Park shouted, his entire body locking tight, as he spurted a load of seed over Tanner's tongue and down his throat. Tanner held on to Park's hips and kept his mouth open to take his first swallow, eagerly tasting every slick pulse of the salty, slightly bitter essence of Park.

When he'd eventually milked the last drop, Tanner swallowed and lapped until Park was clean. Then the beautiful man shivered and Tanner blinked up, suddenly aware that Park might have had different expectations from the blow job.

"Was that okay?" Even as he asked, he realized the question might be a little unnecessary, given the way Park had just shot down his throat and his lazy smile.

Park laughed softly. "I don't know. You might need some more practice." Then he shivered another full body spasm and grinned. "But not quite yet." He patted the mattress. "Why don't you come up here and let me return the favor?"

"Oh— Are you too— Can I—"

"Hey. We can do anything you want." Park reached for his hand to pull him farther up onto the bed. Once again, Tanner covered Park with his bigger body.

"Can I...I want to be inside you again, Park. I mean...if it's okay. Tell me I can have you again."

Park's expression was serious as he caught Tanner's face between his hands while he seemed to search for words. The world ceased to spin for a long moment as fear washed through him at the thought he might have misread the signs.

Pulling their faces together, Park brushed his lips against Tanner's, his warm breath a promise all on its own. "Oh yeah," Park said on a sigh. "I want that, too, honey."

Park stole another kiss, and Tanner's heart pumped fast enough to make his entire body quake. "God. You are so beautiful you take my breath away, Park. I want to get you ready this time. Want to open you."

"You might be a little bit biased given the circumstances," Park said softly. "But yeah, I love your hands on me. The lube is in the nightstand. I left it there just in case..." He pulled in a long breath, then released it on a sigh. "In case you came back. Tanner, honey...I wanted you to come back."

Tanner's inexperience combined with the turmoil that was his life made him susceptible to believing his emotions were grounded in true feelings. Yet Park's words, the way he cradled Tanner's face between his hands...could Park be as monumentally moved by their lovemaking as he was? It felt...right. If nothing else, these last two weeks had given him plenty of time to think, to wish he'd made different choices at so many different moments in his life. Could this be another opportunity he would regret if he let it pass by without comment? He didn't want to think about Park leaving, but he couldn't say what his future would hold—so how he could make promises to anyone.

"I wanted to talk with you...see you. But, Park, I don't deserve—"

Park's mouth opened, but Tanner continued, unwilling to be sidetracked. "Honey—" He tried the endearment on for size and decided he liked it just fine. "Honey, let me talk, just for a minute." Tanner shifted to stretch out alongside Park, then traced his hand over the fine, smooth skin of his chest.

"I have done some monstrously bad things, things I deserve to go to jail for. And just because I'm willing to turn my own family in...I'm going to get away with what I've done. I'm not the kind of person who would ever have interested a man like you and

I'm sure as hell nowhere near the kind of man you deserve."

"Tanner, I'm sure I don't see this the same way you do. Friendship"—he gave Tanner a long look, his wide blue eyes full of emotion—"or love—they can't be earned. They can't be deserved. They just are. I don't care if you want to call it karma or nature, but the truth is out there everywhere. People love who they love."

Tanner's heart was thundering—ready to break free from his self-imposed prison. It suddenly didn't matter how many stern lectures he'd given himself in the past two weeks or the logic he worked to convince himself that Park Williams was a fantasy, a happy memory in an otherwise bleak reality. Could it be possible that Park wanted him—warts and all? Thoughts raced through his mind—his inner caveman apparently ready to lay claim to his man. Tanner stammered partway through what he was almost afraid to ask. "What are you—do you—"

Park smiled a crooked smile. "Yeah, I think maybe I do. Make love to me, Tanner. Please?"

****

Unsure how Tanner would react to his semi-confession of love, Park reached for the nightstand, removed the bottle of lube and a condom, and dropped them on the mattress next to his hip.

He'd never told another man he'd loved him before. Well, technically he still hadn't…unless you counted his father, but that wasn't really the same thing. Plus it had been more than ten years ago, so by all accounts—

"Yes…honey," Tanner said, his voice a low rumble that ground through Park's chest.

"Yes. Let's make love." Tanner sat up and reached for the lube and condom. Taking care of business first, he sheathed himself, then picked up the slick.

Park rolled onto his back and pulled his knees toward his chest, exposing his most intimate part. This might have been Tanner's first time prepping an ass, but there was no hesitancy in his movements. He poured a generous amount of lube on Park's pucker, then traced his fingers over the tight muscle. Park's ass fluttered at the first touch, and he let out a low groan.

Tanner looked up and met his gaze. "Feel good?" he asked, pressing his finger harder against Park's opening, letting the tip slip inside, then back out, spreading the lubrication.

"You have no idea," Park gasped. Tanner's finger slipped in a little further.

"Uhm…yeah. Want to know something?" His voice was a whisper full of secrets and laughter.

"Unh…" Park moaned. He meant yes, but Tanner continued to work his ass with one hand, and the other massaged his perineum before moving on to his balls.

Pushing two fingers inside, Tanner smiled as if he knew exactly what effect he was having on Park. "All those nights alone these last two weeks, I kept thinking about you prepping your ass. It was so fucking sexy to watch…" He grinned, and his fingers found Park's prostate.

"Oh, sweet mother…"

"Mmm…no mothers here, honey. Just me…and I've been practicing."

Park's cock flagged a little. "You've been…" What could he expect? Park was only his first lover. There was no reason to believe he'd be his last. Tanner'd only barely had a taste of sex before he'd been whisked off to goddess knew how many motels, with big burly G-men who toted guns and hard-ons with equal—

"On myself," Tanner finished with a wicked grin.

"Oh, shit, honey. Fuck me now." Park barely recognized his own voice

"That's the idea, lover. Ready?" Tanner shifted to bring his cock closer to Park's entrance before he slipped his fingers out, leaving Park empty, needing.

"Please," he begged. "Need you, honey." Park spread his legs more and lifted his hips, brushing the broad tip of Tanner's cock against his opening. The barely there sensation wasn't nearly enough. He ached to have Tanner fill him, pound him into the mattress—and oh thank god they weren't in a tent, on hard ground because—

"Unh…" he grunted, coming back to the moment. The fingers were back—three from the size of the stretch teasing his opening—slipping inside, twisting…sending Park's channel into a flurry of shivers and spasms.

"More," he panted heavily, meeting Tanner's hungry gaze. The man seemed to be trying to look inside him, to look beyond the raw hunger of the moment and into the very depths of Park's soul. To see the love.

Holding his gaze, Tanner slipped his fingers out, then reached between them to fit the head of his cock to Park's asshole, pushing the tip inside. Park moaned again, and Tanner shook his head, his jaw working as if he was gritting his teeth. He let go of his cock and leaned forward to link their hands together, propping his arms on either side of Park's head. Tanner's mouth closed over his in a rough, possessive kiss, and he sank his penis deep in Park's ass.

He had never felt so full—beyond his ass and into his heart, his soul. Emotions choked into speechlessness as Tanner's cock sat all the way inside Park's body, and he could swear he felt Tanner's heart pulsing through his dick.

Mine. Mine. Mine.

Yours. Yours. Yours.

Tanner shifted on top of Park, somehow finding more space to fill in his rippling passage. Park's channel clutched in a quick series of spasms and Tanner moaned.

"Gotta move, honey," he whispered. "So goddamned beautiful," he said again. Tanner pressed his lips to Park's and started to move his hips, fucking Park, claiming him, embedding himself in every fiber of Park's being.

This was it, everything he'd believed was possible and had hoped to find for himself. The one, true moment in his life where desire and need met love and washed through him, battering away any barriers, leaving him raw.

With self-preservation no longer an option, Park disentangled their fingers and cupped Tanner's face in the gentlest of holds, his heart nearly exploding from the tenderness of their kiss. Pulling his mouth away just long enough to release the words clawing their way up his throat, he whispered into their shared breath.

"Love you, Tanner."

Tanner pulled back enough to study Park's face, his entire face going taut, his eyes darkening with emotion. Hunger and need mixed with hope. "Park," he murmured. He bit his lip and pumped his hips, building the friction between their bodies, brushing the hair on his belly over Park's sensitive cock.

"Park," he repeated, his voice raspy, hoarse. He raised up to his hands, separating their torsos and looking down the length of their bodies. Park followed his gaze and watched as Tanner's thick cock slowly withdrew, then plunged in deep, fast, hard.

As if there was an invisible wire connecting them, Tanner's focus shifted back to Park's face. With their gazes locked, he whispered his name once more. Then Tanner's hips were thrusting, their skin slapping together, his dick rubbing right over Park's prostate. Scorching liquid shot from his dick, coating their stomachs, branding them both.

Needing nothing more than that, Tanner drove his cock balls-deep into Park's channel as his entire body jerked, the muscles of his broad shoulders standing out in stark relief, and he shouted Park's name.

When his hips finally stilled, Tanner lowered himself back to his elbows and plastered his mouth against Park's, a bruising force against his swollen lips. Before he could catch his breath, Tanner eased his cock from Park's ass, then pulled back from the kiss to bury his face in the crook of Park's neck.

"I love you too, Park."

Epilogue

The minute they walked into the living room, long after the dinner hour, Tanner felt the heat crawl up his neck. Shit…this was embarrassing. Not only had he rushed straight into the bedroom to be with Park, they hadn't surfaced from the bed for over twelve hours. Not that it had all been sex—there'd been long lazy naps, nonsense conversations, and, well…more sex. Now that he actually thought about the situation with his big head…he realized their hosts had been very tolerant.

"Well, look who's here," Tyler said in a teasing tone. "I thought I might have to send in some MREs or at least some soy shakes."

Cass hit the television remote, silencing the basketball game, and shifted to face the two of them. "I think they probably had plenty of protein, Ty," Cass said, his voice carrying a smile. "Good to have you back, Tanner. Are you up to talking about what's going on with your situation?"

Park squeezed his hand, and Tanner was simultaneously relieved by the contact and shy about the public display. "You start with the part about the prosecutor, honey, and I'll grab us something to eat. I'll be right back." Park pecked him on the cheek, then strode away, his bare feet peeking out from the frayed hem of his blue jeans.

"Oh, hey, Park—Scooby and Taco are on a walk with Drew and Holden. Little Alex wants to ride Taco, but Drew put the kibosh on that," Ty said with a laugh. Standing quickly, he said, "Hang on, I'll come with you."

"Hah, still don't trust me in your kitchen?" Park said. The playful banter continued as they went toward the hall.

Tanner turned and caught a look on Cass's face as his gaze followed his partner's departing back. Cass faced him at last, a small smile playing on his craggy features. "Sounds like things are going well between you and Park…"

"Yeah, uhm…shit. I'm sorry—"

"I'm not. I think he's going to be very good for you…well, shit. That's pretty damned presumptuous of me. I suppose this could be just a hook up…"

"I…uh…no. It couldn't," Tanner said, his face positively flaming now. He moved to the couch and sat, barely resisting the urge to tug at his shirt collar.

Cass smiled at him. "Good. I'm glad to hear it. Now, tell me what's going on with your case. I know a little from Chance. The federal prosecutor has offered immunity for your testimony?"

"Yes. And a lot of that had to do with you posting the initial bond. Thanks for that, Cass. I could never—"

"Not a worry," Cass cut in. "Did they find all the militia members?"

"Not even close from what I heard. Of course, the prosecutor was disappointed I didn't have more of the member's legal names, just a bunch of stupid nicknames, like T-bone. Maybe that should have been my first clue that I was expendable…I never had a nickname." Tanner laughed but the sound was bitter. "Thomas never had a nickname either—of course he's not talking to me right now. He thinks it's my fault Dad is in jail."

"I think I was able to give the investigators enough on T-bone and the general. Donald Fistus is his real name, by the way. And my dad. He's not doing so good in jail." Tanner swallowed hard, then drew in a deep breath.

"So far, Tim and Dad are holding out, fighting all charges, refusing to acknowledge the feds as having any right to hold them. They think the general is probably in Montana, but it didn't sound like they were having any luck tracking him down."

"Yeah, there's all kinds of survivalists up there. They could work together to keep him hidden for a long time," Cass said.

"Yep. Exactly. And get this…he sent a letter to the president, claiming citizens of his independent nation are being held as prisoners of war and demanding their release."

"Jesus…he really is crazy," Cass said, shaking his head.

"Yeah, I never believed in his politics, Cass, but I should have been more…"

"No more apologizing, honey," Park said as he and Ty stepped back into the room, each carrying a cafeteria-style plastic tray laden with food. Park set his tray on the coffee table, then came to sit on the couch next to Tanner. "You were trying to save your ranch. This escalated far beyond your control."

"Yeah, but that doesn't excuse stupid—and it doesn't do shit to fix what I did to the WSR." Tanner said without meeting Cass's eyes. He didn't know if he would ever be able to look at the big cowboy without an overwhelming sense of guilt. Then the smell of the food hit his nostrils and chased everything else from his mind. He reached for the bowl of popcorn and a bottle of water. "Oh my god, I don't think I realized how hungry I was."

"We might have worked up an appetite," Park said. His smile was broad and the laughter in the blue eyes did interesting things low in Tanner's belly.

Tanner's phone rang, pulling him from the moment before he got embarrassingly lost. Handing his bowl to Park, he stepped away from the couch to take his call. He watched the three men as they chatted…and listened in growing dismay to his attorney. God, he wasn't ready to leave for Flagstaff again so soon. To leave Park.

The men continued to talk amongst themselves as Tanner quietly ended his call. He thought he heard something about kids but he was focused on a more pressing problem. Returning to Park's side, he placed a hand on his lover's thigh while he waited for a break in their conversation.

"The tents arrive Thursday. That gives us two days to get everything set up. Jesse and Drew will take care of the petting zoo and horse rides on Dabney. Whit wants to be in charge of the barn tours, and I don't see why not," Cass said.

"Whit's a good man," Ty said.

"Yeah, he is. And he's damned near as excited as you are about these kids coming. I may have to let him and Chad wrestle over who gets to run the summer camp if this thing goes okay. In fact—"

"Did I hear my name?" Whit said, strolling into the room from the direction of the kitchen. Tanner blinked up at the long, rangy cowboy, noting the damp hair, clean jeans, and stocking feet. The man cleaned up good. The few times he'd seen Whit in Kingman and at rodeos, it seemed strange that a straight man would be working at the WSR—now he wondered if he'd been wrong. Maybe Whit was gay, too.

"Sorry to be a few minutes late, Cass. There was a waiting line for the shower at the bunkhouse. Now what do I have to wrestle over with Chad? And you better hogtie Jesse first—I don't want to get my ass whupped."

Ty barked a laugh. "Jesse could use a good ass whipping."

"Think so, Navy-boy?" Jesse said, sauntering into the room. He was smiling, but the hand that gripped Chad's visibly tightened. "And you"—he nailed Whit with a look—"can keep your hands off my man."

Chad rolled his eyes. "Neanderthal," he said, and elbowed Jesse in the side. The happy grin said he enjoyed Jesse's possessive tone. "Sorry we're late, Cass. Is everyone ready? Or are we still waiting for someone else?"

"No, this is it," Cass replied.

"Petting zoo and tents? We obviously interrupted—should we leave?" Tanner asked.

"It's the Ranch Quest, honey," Park said. "It's what we've been working on while you were in Flag…something Ty put together. A day at the ranch for twenty children and teens. Kids in treatment for life-threatening or terminal illnesses."

"Oh hell. I sort of know about this. My dad—well, let's just say having kids out here was a special sort of trigger for my dad's hate. I'm glad to hear you're going to have the event, given all the trouble out here lately."

"I admit, we thought about cancelling," Ty said, "but with your dad and brother in jail and the general on the run…Chance says he believes the main compound will be safe enough. He and Holden have a bunch of their old law enforcement buddies who volunteered to help with security."

"They wouldn't attack the kids, anyway," Tanner agreed. "That's not the type of publicity they want. Especially if you make it clear that I am not here at the WSR..."

"Not here? Honey, where do you think—" Park started, but another phone ringing interrupted the moment before Tanner had a chance to explain.

"Oh, I got it," Cass said and pushed up from the couch. The old-fashioned desk unit was tucked behind a lamp on a table in the corner of the room. All the WSR hands watched Cass, as if calls on the landline rarely boded well.

"Willow Springs Ranch..." Cass listened for a minute. "Brody? Hey—you doing okay? I saw that shit on television..."

Brody? There was only one Brody who came to mind if you were talking about recent news coverage.

There was a sharp intake of breath, and Tanner glanced over to see Whit's eyes close briefly before his normally easy-going expression covered his quick wince.

Cass continued, "You know you're always welcome here. Standing invite, and normally all the privacy you need. But you should know—we've got an event planned out here this weekend. A small group of sick kids and their caregivers, plus a few parents." There was another pause.

"No press, but still not completely private. And we've had some trouble because the ranch is known for being more than a little gay-friendly. Are you sure this is the best place for you, if you're trying to keep the rumors—"

"This should be interesting," Whit muttered.

"How soon?" Cass turned, his gaze settling on Ty, who nodded once. Question asked and answered between the two lovers. "Yeah, we'll get it set up. See you in the morning."

"Was that really country music boy wonder Brody Kent?" Jesse asked.

"Yep. Seems like the fallout from the three-day celebrity marriage from hell is more than he wants to deal with right now. He's going to stay here for a while. I'll make sure he understands more about Ranch Quest when he gets here. We could always ask Drew and Holden to put him up at their new place. It's a little more secluded than the main compound."

"He can have their old casita, if you want, Cass," Chad said with a shrug. "It's ready."

"Yeah, maybe. Okay, back to the subject at hand—where were we?"

"Actually, Cass, I was just getting ready to tell you all about my phone call," Tanner said. "That was Cade, and they need me back in Flagstaff for a day or two. Again. Jesus, I don't know how I'm ever going to work off my debt to you—but given the timing…"

Park placed a hand on Tanner's leg and looked to Cass. "I've been thinking…I have a friend, okay, more of an acquaintance—actually, I don't even know if I would call him an acquaintance since we've never met, but his heart is in the right place even if he eats meat and uses leather products. Shit that was insensitive, wasn't it? At any rate...several months ago, something happened that had *Shadowman* upset, and he told me a little about this place he lives. I don't think he meant to, he's really private...in fact," Park said.

Tanner didn't miss the look Ty exchanged with Cass when Park finally stopped to breathe. It looked as if they were both holding in a laugh. Park ignored them and continued his thought.

"I don't think he's been back in the chat room since then. We used to meet online a couple of times a week to compare notes about the best places to find food that hasn't been genetically modified. I'm always looking for good sources for organic fruits and vegetables, and *Shadowman* always worried about how corporations were bastardizing the food supply through genetic engineering—especially companies like—"

Cass cleared his throat.

"Oh, right...*anyway*...this place he lives—or lived—is off the beaten track. Sort of a glorified campground with some private cabins right outside Flag. It's called Mountain Shadows. If anyone is looking for Tanner...and you have to admit with the loony tunes general still loose, and an incomplete list of members—and given the current circumstances with the Ranch Quest and Brody Kent…well, it all makes perfect sense, don't you think?" He frowned and took a sip of his water.

"Okay, let me see if I can translate," Tanner said, his voice wavering as he fought his laughter. "You think I should move to this campground to be closer to Flagstaff and harder to find so I don't draw any more trouble to the WSR." The thought others could be hurt sobered him quickly enough. "I actually think the idea is a good one, except I need to work off—"

"You will, in time, Tanner," Cass interrupted. "For now, your job is to help get this group behind bars. Even if the feds don't think the case merits protective custody—and by the way, neither does Chance—making you harder to find is a good idea. Your safety is more important than trying to fix the past."

"Not just you, either—if you'll have us," Park added quietly.

Tanner turned, certain the surprise was written all over his face. Or maybe relief. Or hope. Whatever…all he knew was Park wanted to come with him.

"I thought you—" He looked around the room, noticed the smiles on the faces of the men. He cleared his throat. "Ranch Quest?" he managed to ask.

"I don't belong here, Tanner. I was already set to leave, until I found out you were on your way."

"You stayed for me?" Tanner whispered.

"Oh, honey, if you didn't figure that out, I must not have been trying hard enough…" Park said, then leaned in to steal a kiss.

Cass cleared his throat, and Tanner jerked his head back before they spontaneously combusted right here on the couch.

"Okay, now that we have that cleared up, Tanner, you and Park go pack and I'll call Cade to set up this…Mountain Shadows?" Cass said.

"Pack hell, they need to put out the damned fire first," Ty said with a laugh. "I'll take you into Kingman for the van tomorrow, Park, then you can head out whenever you're ready."

Park stood and tugged on Tanner's hand. "Come on, let's sort out the details."

"Hey, that's a good idea…I think we need to sort out some details, too, Chad," Jesse said with a snort.

"Not until we're done planning," Chad said and pushed Jesse back onto the couch.

Tanner was vaguely aware of the conversation continuing, but he was already dragging Park down the hall—and toward their very unexpected future.

****

Stopping on their way out of Mohave County at the campsite where they'd first met had seemed like a good idea. After all, they'd been in a desperate hurry to leave. Tanner had always intended to come back, to retrieve the rest of Park's belongings, to set the site back to its natural state. They'd left behind the tent, sleeping bags, in fact, nearly everything. Tanner had carried a bag with clothing and a backpack, while Park had his hands full of overexcited Chihuahua and they'd run like hell. Now, Tanner stood with his hands on his hips and tried to pretend the scene in front of them wasn't devastating, but that would be a lie.

The bent and blackened frames of the camp chairs and tent protruded at odd angles from the circle of stones of the fire ring. The ice chest had been hacked into pieces and was also partially burned. The sleeping bags had been sliced open, and bits of stuffing clung to the Manzanitas and lower tree branches. Everywhere you looked, evidence of a destructive fit of rage.

"T-bone," Tanner whispered.

Strong arms wrapped around his waist, then Park leaned in against his back, just holding tight.

"Most likely," Park agreed. His voice was easy enough, and the hint of his smile seemed to carry right through Tanner.

Stepping away from the embrace, Tanner turned to face Park. Today, his long hair spilled around his shoulders, framing his face, making his blue eyes seem even bigger than usual. He'd watched him in the bathroom mirror as Park had put on his makeup, marveling at the steady hand as the narrow pencil lined his lids. He wanted to trace his hands over the high cheekbones, the straight nose, the pouty-full bottom lip. He was the most beautiful man Tanner had ever seen. Park deserved so much better.

"Why are you coming with me? You don't even know me." The words escaped before Tanner could draw them back. "I'm not a good person…you deserve so much better."

"Tanner, don't. Let's not worry about the past. We can't change it, right?" Park's smile faltered a bit, before sliding away, his expression turned serious. "Honey, you don't know me either. And that's the fun of this adventure. We can spend all the time we need to get to know each other. We can share our secrets and make new memories."

"But what do we have in common?"

"Besides the hot monkey sex, you mean, right? Because I have to tell you, that blow job in the shower this morning was hot…you're a fast learner." Park's laughter rang out, the smile returned full force.

"Shut up," Tanner laughed as his face heated at the memory of the shower sex. Of him on his knees as the water beat down on his back, while Park's cock pushed into his throat. He shook off the mental image before he got lost. "But yeah, since you brought it up—"

"—so to speak," Park interrupted.

"Dammit, Park, I'm trying to be serious here. And I'm trying to give you a graceful way out, now that we've left the WSR. Look at this." He waved his hand at the campsite that now resembled a garbage dump. "Yeah, my brother most likely did it. This time. But

171

you said it yourself, there's no guarantee they won't try again. If something happens to you because of me—"

"When will you get it through your thick head that not everything is your fault? If a meteor landed on my head, would you try to own that, too?"

Tanner snorted. "No, but—"

"Exactly…no buts. I want to know you. I want to know the man who can pull out a Star Trek reference in the middle of a fight. I want to know the man who worries about my dogs, and doesn't complain when one hundred and seventy-five pounds of wannabe lapdog climbs onto his chair. I want to know the man who can fuck my brains out then turn me over and make sweet gentle love. There is just so much I want to learn about who you are. Please, Tanner—say we can have this time. Don't try to throw it away for misplaced guilt. The Fates brought us together for a reason, honey. I'm pretty sure you're stuck with me."

Swallowing hard against the tightness in his throat, Tanner looked down at Park and knew he was lost. There was no way he could do anything other than whatever this man asked of him. They would figure this out. "Yeah. Okay. Whatever you want, Park. I promise I'll try."

Then he turned away and cleared his throat. "Let's pick this shit up and get out of here. I think I've had enough of this part of Arizona."

Without saying anything else, Park handed Tanner a large plastic bag, and the two of them circled the site, picking up as much of the trash as they could. Scooby and Taco got into the spirit and raced ahead, tails wagging, as they sniffed at both real and imaginary debris.

"What is this?" Tanner asked, snatching at something white, nearly buried underneath the soft dirt at the base of the juniper trees. The paper was dirty, the pencil drawing faded, but the talent was clear.

Park looked over and flushed. "Oh, uh…" He tried to snatch the paper from Tanner's hand, but he pulled it back.

"This is me…"

"Yeah. Well, you and Taco and Scoobs. I know I probably should have asked, but the three of you were so sweet lying together that first afternoon. Once I carried everything down from the van, I took a little break and watched you sleep. That's no big deal," he said and tried to reach for the paper again.

"Do you do this a lot? Draw, I mean?"

"Mmm…I do some. I like to sketch out my ideas sometimes before I put the paint to canvas."

"You paint, too? Why didn't I know this?"

Park shrugged and bent to pick up the last of the sleeping bag filling that was caught on the juniper bark. "It just hasn't come up yet, Tanner. It would have once we get to Flag. I need to hit the art store to replace my supplies."

"What happened to your—"

"Most of my supplies were in the van. I tried to recover them but the damage was…well, it just wasn't worth it. Besides most of that crap was old or not what I really needed. It's just something I do, no big deal." Park flushed and looked away…not normal behavior for the typically blunt man. All of Tanner's inner warning bells went on high alert.

"What aren't you telling me?" he asked.

Park's cheeks were a bright red when he turned to face Tanner once again. "I painted a lot when I was working for CPS. It relieved some of the stress but the paintings started to get…dark. Depressing. It's one of the reasons I needed to quit."

"All this and a painter, too," Tanner said, shaking his head, smiling at the flustered Park.

"I used to think I could be an artist. You know, for a living. Sell my paintings to unsuspecting tourists or the NY Metropolitan…whichever came first."

"And all those paintings were destroyed in the van?" Tanner asked, trying not to show his dismay.

"Oh, hell no," Park said. "Between the dogs and the gear, there wasn't that kind of space. I've got a storage room in Flag. I've got all kinds of stuff stored there. More clothes, most of my paintings and pottery, a jumbo-sized dog bed," he said and smiled toward Taco.

Dropping his bag to the ground, Tanner closed the distance between them and wrapped his arms around the smaller man, just before he mashed their mouths in a hot kiss. Their tongues slid together, the taste already familiar, intoxicating. As necessary as breathing. He was overwhelmed by the knowledge that something so important to Park hadn't been lost completely.

Still keeping one arm around Park, Tanner broke their kiss. "I don't know shit about art—"

"But you know what you like…" Park teased with a smile.

"Yeah, I do, so let me finish, Park. I'm putting away my thoughts of owning the Trip-T. It's gone. Even if the government doesn't claim the ranch, I'm going to sell my share of it—there are just too many bad memories associated with this part of the state, with the stuff my family did. I'm ready to move on.

"But you…your dream of being an artist? Why not give it a real shot?" Tanner held up the sketch. "This is…well, I think it's good. I want to see your paintings. I want to give you something back for believing in me." He stroked Park's face, and got lost for a minute in his lover's eyes. Park started to lean closer, but Tanner wasn't finished.

"As soon as we get to Flag, I'm going to see those trustee lawyers and get my money. Then we're going to the art store and I'm going to buy you everything. You have to let me replace it all, to give you all the supplies you need. Then you can spend every day following your dream, giving it a real effort—not squeezing it in after work. Please?"

Park's eyes took on a sheen, and it was his turn to swallow hard. "Yes," he whispered. "Yes," he said again, loud enough to cause the dogs to race to them. "Yes," he shouted, laughing hard. The dogs started to bark and dance a circle around the two of them.

Picking up both trash bags in one hand, Tanner grabbed Park's hand and started pulling him toward the road, practically running before he'd taken two steps. "Come on…let's hurry."

Park laughed harder, but allowed himself to be dragged along. "Hey," he choked out. "Shouldn't we have a celebratory blow job or something?"

Tanner stopped so abruptly, Park slammed into him with a grunt. "Yes…blow job," he murmured. Then he shook his head. "Not here…I need to get out of this place. I want to start over. With you. Let's go home."

With a loud whoop, Park tightened their joined hands. "Now that's better than a cosmic Creamsicle. I agree. Let's go home."

~~The End~~

About the Author

Raised in California, Laura likes it hot, which explains why she ended up in Arizona via such diverse places as Japan, Maine, and Florida, and many more places in between. After retiring from the US Navy, she found a niche working for land management agencies, including the National Park Service and the Bureau of Land Management. Though she has held many jobs around the world, her favorite was working and living in Grand Canyon National Park. Working (and eating) in New Orleans was a close second. You will find many of her books are set against the rich backdrops provided by coastal Louisiana and northern Arizona.

When asked how she started writing, Laura tells of waking on Boxing Day a few years ago, with a woman named Elena MacFarland yammering in her dreams, demanding her story be told. Despite never attempting to write fiction before that morning, Laura ignored all of the holiday visitors and the Highland Destiny series was born. She doesn't believe it was a coincidence that the great grandmother who died when Laura was just a baby was named Elena MacFarland. Destiny does play a hand.

Laura became a full-time writer in 2012, and now she spends her time writing, watching her Arizona Diamondbacks, and working on her very own version of the Willow Springs Ranch in northwestern Arizona. She is a multi-published author of erotic romance, mystery, and urban fantasy and her books can be found at all major online retailers.

Connect with Laura at:

Twitter: *@LauraHarner*

Facebook: *facebook.com/lauraharner*

Or even better…check out the website at: *LauraHarner.com*

Also Available

Forbidden Love

Detective Danielle Delacroiux is one kick-ass detective with the Généreux PD, and she's got a murder on her hands. By all accounts, Crease Martin was nothing but a homeless drunk and a lousy informant, but Dani counted him as one of hers. Now she'll stop at nothing to find his murderer. With a red silk handkerchief under the body as her first clue, Dani wants a quick break. When a handsome stranger practically strolls up to the crime scene, Dani can't help but notice his expensive Italian suit, red silk tie, and empty breast pocket. Could he be who she's looking for?

Dani is less than impressed when Mr. tall, dark, and yummy is introduced as the newest lawyer in town, and even worse, he's another of the Charbonnet offspring. The deadly feud between the Delacroiux and Charbonnet families goes way back, and there is one thing she knows without a doubt. If Hawk Charbonnet committed this crime, she'll be damned if his connections will do him any good. She'll happily lock his arrogant ass in jail for the rest of his life. Which would be a shame, because she had to admit, it was a fine-looking ass.

~*~

Part of Me

Jason's life hasn't been easy. Feeling responsible for the death of his twin the night they graduated from high school, Jason commits emotional suicide by revealing he's gay after his brother's funeral, permanently severing all ties with his ultra-conservative parents. But when he runs to Hunter Dane for comfort, all he can see is the same rejection mirrored on his best friend's face.

Twelve years later, Jason needs all the support he can get to beat back the cancer invading his body. When Hunter unexpectedly shows up to shift from former friend to caregiver, Jason must battle his attraction even while he's waging the biggest fight of his life.

~*~

Altered States, free prologue for the Altered States Series

New Orleans Police Detective Sam Garrett can't believe his bad luck when he's assigned to investigate a string of gay-bashings turned deadly in the French Quarter. Especially when he realizes Travis Boudreaux, his new, hot, and most-likely-straight partner, plans to use him as bait. The worst part? They've got no back-up because the rest of the city is preoccupied by another series of killings — the victims drained of blood.

~*~

Deep Blues Goodbye, Book One of the Altered States Series

The world might not have been ready for vampires when NOPD Detective Travis Boudreaux had the bad taste to sit up at his own funeral, but two years later, the new cause célèbre is civil rights for preternatural beings and most humans are on the bandwagon. Except whoever is killing vampires and wannabes.

Detective Sam Garrett hates all things preternatural. Having your undead partner try to make you his first meal will do that to a guy. One final screw-up gets Sam banished to the Paranormal Criminal Investigations Unit—the Odd Squad— under the oversight of Detective Danny Burkette.

Now it's up to Burkette to work with Garrett by day and Boudreaux by night as they follow a trail of clues that leads from the historic cemeteries of New Orleans to the bayous of southern Louisiana. Under the all-too-interested gaze of a Master vampire and the local werewolf pack Alpha, they discover some lessons in life—and death—take longer to learn...and not all second chances are created equal.

Warning: In this series the vampires don't sparkle, werewolves kill, and sometimes the men have sex. With each other.

~*~

Ty Hard, Book One of the Willow Springs Ranch Series

Tyler has used Don't Ask, Don't Tell as a shield against the truth since he was seventeen. Now, Ty finds himself cut loose from his Navy career after months of rehab from a debilitating head injury. At a loss as to what to do with his life, he travels to Willow Springs Ranch in Arizona to visit his surrogate father, only to arrive minutes after his oldest friend's death. Ty must come to terms with the loss while he fights to keep the PTSD from pulling him under. The last thing he's ready to think about is his growing attraction for another man.

Rancher Cass Cartwright's relationships never last more than a few hours, and that's just the way he likes it. Now he's in danger of doing the one thing he swore never to do: fall in love. Can Cass convince Ty to let go of his past or will sabotage at the ranch kill their love before it has a chance to grow?

~*~

Hold Tight, Book Two of the Willow Spring Ranch Series

Sheriff Holden Titus had organized his fresh start down to the last detail. Except for the part about the bomb that blew his plans all to hell. Now he's running out of time, without a job, without a home, and struggling to get back on his feet. Literally.

Despite the impolite rejection, Drew knows he didn't have the wrong impression months ago when he asked the sheriff to dance, but he never expected to have Holden's life in his hands. Literally.

Thanks to some meddlesome matchmaking, the two men are now temporary housemates at the Willow Springs Ranch and Drew is determined to help Holden heal, both physically and emotionally. Even if it means he has to drag the other man kicking and screaming to physical therapy...and out of the closet. In fact, that might be kind of fun.

The problem is, Holden doesn't consider himself in the closet...but not all secrets are created equal.

~*~

Oceans Apart, Book Two of the Separate Ways Series

It's been two years since Lord Jamie Mainwaring and Detective Remy Remington worked and loved their way through their one and only case before going their separate ways.

Now Jamie is once again mixing agency business with pleasure as he and his partner, Agent Ryan Whiteside, are assigned to a case involving piracy in the Caribbean.

Remy and his old friend Miggy are still detectives, but they've gone private in Phoenix. When their biggest client sends them to supervise an unusual diamond transfer, they think their toughest challenge will be maintaining their cover as a gay couple on a barefoot-style cruise.

When murder connects the dots between the two cases, the four men must learn to work together as relationships and loyalties are tested amid misunderstandings and memories on the high seas.

www.ingramcontent.com/pod-product-compliance
Lightning Source LLC
Chambersburg PA
CBHW030253130626
46549CB00002B/512